Being Human

A NOVEL BY

C. NIELSEN TAYLOR

For Elliot,
Invincible soul
So much inspiration —

writeallalong@yahoo.com

Printed in the United States of America.

Word Project Press, Sonora, CA

www.wordprojectpress.com

Book Layout and Design by Melody Baker
Illustration by Art Theisen

SBN-13: 978-0989068284
ISBN-10: 0989068285

This book may be purchased in bulk for educational, promotional or business purposes. Please direct all inquiries to:
writeallalong@yahoo.com.

First Edition September 2015

10 9 8 7 6 5 4 3 2 1

For my parents,
who entrusted me to the natural world
without hesitation . . .

And for my grandsons, Cole and Chase.

PREFACE

I was raised down a dirt road in the midst of acres of orange trees, and as a child was regularly told to "go outside and play." The flora and fauna were my primary companions – my toys, eucalyptus leafs and pods, scissor plants and rocks – a stick horse with no embellishment. There were dangers: a cement stand pipe I had been warned against but lowered myself into and lived not to tell – a slow walk through a double line of hives to test Dad's theory that bees only stung if a person was afraid.

Nature was my home; I was fascinated by life and pretty much fearless – then I went to kindergarten. I had never seen a children's book, a crayon or a pair of blunt scissors before I entered school. Sitting at a table while other children colored and cut construction paper into the basic shapes, I stared out the window at a huge stand of eucalyptus. When I wiggled during nap time, the teacher put me behind the piano. I began to develop coping mechanisms, and as I ventured further into this novel I saw that it was, in many ways, an exploration of my experience of becoming a "civilized" human being.

The story is not finished; my characters will continue to grow. I'm curious to see what doors will open, which will close and what paths they will choose. My wish is that others, especially the younger of us, begin to explore more fully the human frailty of "casting fate to the wind" and giving our "internal con-artists" the reins. We can choose, instead, to respect ourselves, each other and the intricate, interdependent web of all life on planet Earth.

– C.N.T, August, 2015

ACKNOWLEDGMENTS

It took a village to complete this novel. Many thanks to: Ella Baxter, Sheila Bender, Joan Canty, Royce Cornett, Peter Demartini, Cale Fanucchi, Shaun Herbst, Noreen Parks, Pamela Pickup, Josh and Maya Roe, Ilena Rosenthal, Cassie Ross, Ellen Stewart, Samantha and Gary Stewart, Meryl Soto, Kim Warren, Jonathan Weldon and Write on Women of Sonora, CA.

A special thanks to Eli Taylor, who shared my enthusiasm for the concept of this book, encouraged me from the beginning and was present at the very moment I was able to say, "I'm done, I'm really done!" And to Jim Angle, who had doubts about the concept but asked to read a few chapters then called to say he wanted to read more. These two dear men propelled me to the finish line, and I am truly grateful. And to Art Theisen, who put pictures to words and turned my thoughts more clearly to the sequel.

And to Sam . . . where would I be without you.

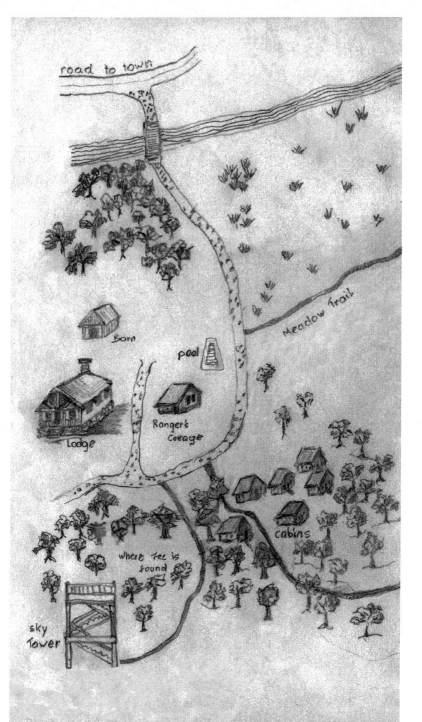

John Muir
Environmental Camp

ANCIENT REDWOOD FELLED - COUPLE DIES

Saturday, June 10, 2000

Scotia, CA – Holly Angle, 27, and her partner Lyle Stone, 30, were killed early yesterday morning when an old growth redwood was felled by Electric California, Inc. According to Humboldt county sheriff, Bud Barnett, the couple had attempted to save the ancient tree by residing on a ten by ten foot platform slung between its branches since Thanksgiving Day, 1998.

After several postings in the immediate area and announcements through a bullhorn, the tree, along with several others, was felled at dawn. Workman said they had no idea the couple was in the tree at the time. "We gave them plenty of warning" William Guest, project foreman, told reporters. "We thought they were gone."

When informed of the accident, Angle's mother, Deborah Bartell of San Jose, reported her daughter had likely given birth in the past few weeks. "She asked a friend for information on home birth several months ago," Bartell told reporters. "I crocheted a blanket for the baby. It was blue, Holly's favorite color; her friend told me she would make sure she got it." Officials at the scene said Ms. Angle was not pregnant and no infant was found.

Protesters are planning a massive rally on the steps of the capitol in Sacramento to demand that Governor Gray Davis keep his campaign promise to ban old-growth logging and to launch a thorough investigation into the deaths of Angle and Stone.

What is man without beasts? If all beasts were gone,
Men would die from great loneliness of spirit,
For whatever happens to the beasts, also happens to man.
All things are connected. Whatever befalls the earth
Befalls the children of the earth.

. . . Chief Seattle

CHAPTER ONE

August 31, 2012

They entered the cavern in order of tradition: feline first, followed by bear, fowl and deer; raccoon and coyote flanked the opening. The Council had been summoned for an emergency meeting. After years of successful transitions, they had been confident that today would signal the completion of the first phase of The Plan – And yet, the air was filled with sober speculation on what might have gone wrong.

In the beginning, the boy had been delivered to Black Oak Forest as a swaddled infant dangling from Condor's powerful beak. Today he had come full circle, returning to the same forest on the cusp of manhood. He was healthy, impeccably skilled in the way of many creatures and, after twelve times round the seasons, ready for reintroduction to his own species.

The Council turned its attention to Doe. In silent communion, she shared her experience of the boy's arrival that morning. They saw her retrieve the sky-colored second skin he had been wrapped in when Condor brought him to her as an infant, and felt the jump of her heart when the boy, so different from the chubby toddler she remembered, raced into the clearing. It had been nine years since she and Buck had seen him, but the scent was true.

This afternoon Buck bounded from the clearing with the boy on his back, their destination a heavily wooded area near a group of human dens. Buck should have returned hours ago. Where was he? The question ran through packs and dens, through flocks and burrows – Nothing – Some reported hearing a shot ricochet through the hills. Had Buck fallen? . . . And where, they wondered, was the boy?

**

Condor had facilitated all of the boy's relocations and, as with each transition, it was imperative this last one be implemented unnoticed by humans. So far that had been relatively easy, but this time humans were sure to be nearby. Landing in the clearing had been risky – taking off from flat ground was a bit of an ordeal. Still, he had descended, ever so briefly, to envelop the boy in his tremendous wings. Moments later, he made his way aloft to witness Buck leave the clearing with the boy on his back.

He lingered, now, at the top of a yellow pine to wait for confirmation of the boy's reintroduction. Soon the great vulture would embark on the long journey home where he would rest and celebrate with his human colleague.

The final creature tribe to mentor the boy was a herd of Big Horn Sheep living on the east side of the Sierra-

Nevada Mountains. Two years of survival at high elevation in the cold, dry, windy climate had honed a razor-sharp, sure-footed, nearly inexhaustible endurance in the boy. Using the sweeping shadow of Condor's nine-foot wing span as guide, he had maintained a steady pace, due west, over sheer granite peaks on their return to Black Oak Forest.

The Council had instructed the herd to prepare the boy for reintroduction by chewing away his waist-length hair. Now, it stood out from his head like dry thistle to reveal a newly angular visage and a lithe, muscular body. From a hundred feet above, the vulture could see the cluster of letters on the boy's right thigh, the identifying mark Condor had instructed a woodpecker to tattoo on the child before he was transferred from Buck and Doe's care. What seemed large and bold all those years ago was diminutive and faint by comparison, but it was there. RRAB – Condor alone knew the meaning.

Huddled on a granite precipice on their last night together, Condor had shared his own experience of returning to his natural habitat, the thrill and challenge of answering the call of one's own species. Hatched and raised by humans, Condor was reintroduced as part of a cohort, a clutch of condors his own age. Together, they had spread their wings and dropped off a cliff into a current exactly as their ancestors had done for 12,000 years.

But the boy would be alone. He must adapt to a world his ancestors could never have imagined. Soon, he would encounter human language. Condor had been exposed daily to this form of communication by the humans who raised him. Over the years, in an attempt to prepare the boy for the complexities of human speech, he thought in word sounds while visualizing their meaning.

As they watched the sun disappear, Condor knew the time had come for him to explain that humans could speak false, a skill no creature knew.

What is speak false? the boy wondered.

It is a decoy, like a bird dragging a wing to divert attention from its nest. It is a trick, a distraction; the bird means no harm. But speak false can be a threat. Stay alert.

How will I know?

Watch the eyes.

CHAPTER TWO

Dan Fisk felt like a lucky man. He'd worked as river guide, federal park ranger and, for the past eight years, as head naturalist/year-round caretaker of John Muir Environmental Camp. Wiry, fit, and nearly forty, his favorite mode of transportation was his trusty bicycle. The old camp pickup stayed parked for such long periods of time he'd developed the habit of disconnecting the battery between his infrequent trips to the nearest town some thirty-five miles away.

There were two six-week camping sessions each summer, the first for girls, the second for boys. Tomorrow, the second session was coming to a close; the last of the campers would be leaving. He would miss them, especially those who shared his enthusiasm for nature's endless wonders. He found himself grinning as he recalled Alex Perry running up to him earlier in the day shouting, "Ranger Dan, I just saw a condor!"

Undoubtedly, Alex had spotted an extra large turkey vulture coasting on the currents above camp. Not wanting to dampen the boy's enthusiasm, he told Alex he would do some investigating. Besides, it would give him a reason to contact Sonja Henderson. Last he'd heard she was monitoring the reintroduction of California condors in Los Padres National Forest.

Returning from nightly cabin check, Dan took a cool shower then stretched out on his bed in the small rustic cottage he called home. This time tomorrow would be the start of nine months of solitude. He was looking forward to some peace and quiet ... well, hopefully. He'd heard rifle shots close by this afternoon. Deer season was a long way off, and hunting any time of year was strictly prohibited on camp property. Most likely guys doing target practice, but if he heard it again, he'd have to ferret out who was responsible and play the tough guy.

Eyes growing heavy, he listened to a moth beat its wings against the screen door. At least once a summer a camper would ask him why light drew bugs; it proved to be a good opening to talk about man's inventions and their effect on even the smallest creatures. "Moths," he would tell them, "are disoriented by artificial light. They have evolved to use celestial light, the sun, moon and stars for navigation. When the source of light is nearby, the insect tries to maintain a constant angle to that source, causing it to spiral toward the light. The attraction is sometimes deadly."

**

The boy scanned the horizon from a high branch of ponderosa pine. As dusk faded to dark, he noticed unusual flickers in the distance, like stars, but oddly close to the ground. He ignored the temptation to investigate. Tonight, he would sleep in an abandoned heron nest in a branch above, but first he must return to the ground below.

The Council and his mentors had prepared him for this day with diligence and care. Guided by Condor's shadow, he had sprinted toward his future without hesitation. Mounting Buck's back with confidence, he'd been eager to join his own kind, to learn their ways, and fulfill his destiny as mediator between creature and human being. But in an instant, the exhilarating momentum had come to an abrupt end.

There had been no warning, just a quick, piercing sound, and suddenly he was catapulted over Buck's massive horns. He'd scrambled to his feet and looked back to see the great stag collapsed on the ground, legs jerking, still trying to run. Kneeling beside the motionless head, he'd looked deep into the eyes of his first teacher; the message there was clear . . . *I am leaving. My spirit is with you . . . my body will give you strength. Have no fear; you are close to your destination . . .* The eyes had grown cloudy, one last breath, one shuddering sigh – and then he heard human voices for the very first time.

The multiplicity of sounds the humans produced was unlike anything the boy had heard before, but he understood the implication of the tone – Conflict. Instantly, his body was saturated with adrenalin and he'd scurried up the pine to safety. Moments later, two adult males appeared below, the larger one still growling fiercely. The smaller, and obviously younger of the two, cowered and began to dig a hole while the other slit the underside of Buck's body with a long shiny stone. Together they had pulled the viscera free, flung it into the hole and covered it with dirt and rock. Then the hole-digger sat at the base of the pine and the other walked away into the forest.

Later he'd heard a rumbling sound and was astounded when the source of the noise came into view. It had stopped near Buck's body, fell silent, and the larger human climbed out of it – A Moving Den! The two hoisted Buck's carcass onto its back, climbed inside, and hunters and prey rolled away in a cloud of foul smelling smoke.

Now, as the sun began to fade, the boy lowered himself to the ground. Head raised, nostrils open, ears and eyes keenly attuned, he crawled to the mound of dirt and rock. The scent of blood intensified as he set the rocks aside and clawed through the shallow layer of earth. Slipping a hand beneath the mass, he felt the strange skin Doe had given him before he climbed onto Buck's back ... *The human makes a second skin. This was yours when you were brought to me.*

The color of the second skin was no longer the color of a clear sky; soaked in blood and covered with dirt, he recognized it now by the odd texture. After carefully separating the heart and liver from the mass, he reburied the rest then wrapped the precious nutrients in the second skin ... *My body will give you strength* ... He had completed Buck's final instruction – What now?

Squatting next to the mound, the boy's jaw began to tremble; a debilitating quake surged through his body. In an effort to stop the shaking, he inhaled deeply, again and again until the distinctive scent of Black Oak Forest pulled him back in time, setting him awash with memories unbidden: at first only sound, *an excruciating buzz, his own terrified infant wail, the whoosh of powerful wings* – then distinct physical

18

sensations, *swinging through space, aching cold, violent shaking . . . and all at once, a miraculous calm . . . his face pressed to Doe's belly, suckling warm milk.*

As the tremors dissipated, the boy relaxed onto his back to welcome what other recollections might come: *Clutching the smooth horns of Buck's lowered head, he stands upright. Buck moves slowly backward, and he takes his first tentative steps . . . Scraping a knee, he cries out; Doe covers his mouth with her own, pushes breath into his lungs, teaches him to be silent . . . older now, he tumbles with Feline's cubs, feasts on fresh kill . . .*

Today, he has learned that humans, too, seek the nourishment of flesh.

When the spell of the past was finally broken, the most basic requirement of all living things demanded the boy's attention, and the faint sound of water tumbling over rock drew him to stream's edge. After drinking his fill, he devoured a portion of Buck's liver. Then he turned to face the full moon . . . and a long mournful howl echoed through Black Oak Forest.

CHAPTER THREE

Nine a.m., ninety degrees. The campers had finished breakfast and were rolling up their sleeping bags for the last time. An end of season swim party would start right after lunch. Until then, the boys were free to roam as long as they stayed on the trails. Poison oak made that restriction fairly easy to enforce. The misery of an oozing, itching rash was no joke.

"Hey Alex, throw me some of your pit stick. I'm sweatin' already." Alex threw his deodorant to Josh and finished packing clothes into his duffel.

"Old Spice, now that's class," Josh said. He tossed the container onto Alex's bunk, then proposed a plan for their last few hours at camp. "Let's take the meadow trail to the stream, practice the native walk, see if we can sneak up on some animals there."

Alex knew they weren't going to spot wildlife this time of day, but he agreed anyway. At least they could take one last dip in the swimming hole.

When they reached the meadow, Josh turned, held a

finger to his lips and began walking slowly down the dusty trail. Antsy to reach the shady woods, Alex took off running. Josh attempted to catch up, but it was useless. Alex had proved to be the fastest runner at camp, the fastest swimmer, too. He was sitting in the shade grinning when Josh collapsed beside him.

Alex stood up. "Now," he said, "let's practice the native walk." They started into the forest, minding each step as they moved toward one of the few places where the stream was more than knee deep.

**

In the morning the boy left the pine carrying his nourishment with him. Moving silently through the forest, he returned to the stream to anchor his food in cool water. The cradle of sticks atop the huge pine hadn't allowed for much sleep. Now, he settled himself comfortably on a wide horizontal branch of a live oak where the dense foliage made him virtually invisible. A gentle breeze cooled and soothed; finally, he was able to relax enough to attune his mind and heart to Doe's searching. But the connection was interrupted all too soon by a repugnant odor and the unmistakable rhythm of two two-legged creatures approaching downwind.

**

"Last one in is a rotten egg," Alex shouted, as he and Josh neared the swimming hole.

"Jeez, Alex, what's up with you? I thought we were going to sneak up on some animals."

"We're too late for that." Alex shucked his shoes, peeled off all of his clothes and plunged into the water. "Come on, dude; cool off."

Josh removed his shoes and tested the water with bare feet. "I think I'll wait for the pool party."

Alex flung water in Josh's direction until Josh finally relented and waded in. They splashed and wrestled, challenged each other to a breath holding contest, then sat on the bank and talked about girls and school.

"I had a girlfriend before I left," Alex said, "but who knows if she'll still be interested when I get home."

"Yeah, lots of stuff can change over the summer. I got a letter from my mom. Dad could be gone by the time I get back. He might have to go out of state for work."

Alex tossed a rock into the water. "That's the story of my life. My dad spends most of his time in Washington, D.C."

"Oh, yeah, he's a congressman or something, isn't he?"

"Uh huh. Mom hates Washington, so we hardly ever go. That's fine by me."

**

The interruption of his connection with Doe was troubling to the boy, but what followed was an engrossing display of human interaction. With a clear view of the stream, he was witness to two young males frolicking like baby otters. Their shouts, and the softer modulation of tone they made while sitting on the bank, fascinated him. But when he focused his attention on the bodies themselves, he felt unsettled, apprehensive – it was true.

I am the same . . . I am *human . . .*

And for the first time in his life . . . he lost his balance.

**

"Did you hear that?" Alex twisted around to scan the slope behind them, sweeping his eyes across the oak where the boy, suspended by one hand, held perfectly still.

Josh grabbed his shoes. "Something's giving me the creeps. Let's go back."

"You go on," Alex said. "I'll catch up."

"Suit yourself." Josh put on his shoes and headed back toward the meadow.

Alex dressed then moved cautiously up the slope above the bank. He was positive he'd heard something falling in one of the trees. Whatever it was, it was large – and it hadn't hit the ground.

**

Pulling himself back onto the thick branch, the boy stretched his body out to conform to the limb's landscape. Shadowed by leaves, his tan skin and dull hair blended seamlessly with the tree's bark. Soon, the shorter of the two humans left the way they had come, but the other put on his second skin and foot coverings and walked straight uphill.

**

Alex surveyed the trees before him: two, thickly needled pines, a substantial live oak, a few smaller trees and seedlings. Avoiding thick patches of the dreaded poison oak, he walked to the base of one of the pines and, recalling how long it took him to spot a heron nest Dan had shown the campers earlier that summer, gazed up into the branches for a long time. After doing the same at the second pine, he turned toward the live oak. Its small leaves were much denser than the needles of the pines, but once under their cover, the broad horizontal limbs might reveal something of interest.

**

The young human stood at the base of two nearby pines, scanning the branches of each one before turning toward the oak. The boy flattened himself against the limb, but before shifting completely out of the line of sight, he looked closely at the curious face coming toward him. The eyes were the color of the sky, the color of the second skin doe had given him. Could his own eyes be the color of the sky?

Pondering . . .

When footsteps signaled the stalker's retreat, the boy prepared to resume his connection with Doe by taking a long deep breath; the lingering scent of the human filled his nostrils. His body reacted to the pungent odor with the convulsing sneeze and by the time he recovered, the stalker was rushing back toward the tree.

Sound had betrayed him, but the boy could tell this human relied heavily on sight. His nostrils did not flare, nor did his ears tilt in auditory investigation. Mesmerized, he stared at the face, at the darting, sky colored eyes; the pull was magnetic, inevitable – Contact.

The boy did not flinch. Without so much as a blink, he searched to see what lay behind those sky-colored eyes.

**

Alex's heart stopped – EYES! Eyes without context, eyes suspended like the Cheshire Cat of Alice in Wonderland; but these were not the eyes of a cat. These eyes looked almost . . . human. Some native peoples considered bears to be their cousins. Was that because bear eyes look human? If it is a bear, it must be a baby or, surely, he'd be able to see more than those intense, unblinking eyes . . . And where there's a baby bear, there's a mama bear ready to defend her young.

Alex ran.

**

The boy carefully examined the human footprints on the muddy bank, then put his own foot on top of the pattern. His feet were significantly wider, his toes longer and, unlike his own, there was no trace of claws. The unpleasant odor had faded to a tolerable level; he may *be* human, but he did not *smell* human. Following the prints to the edge of the meadow, he climbed to the top of a tall cedar and settled there to wait and watch.

**

The pool deck was jammed. Sodas and chips sat on a large table next to a barbecue where hot dogs and hamburgers sizzled on the grill. The aroma was enticing, but Alex jogged right past, reaching the cottage just as Dan stepped out the door.

"Hey, you're going the wrong way," Dan said. "There's a party going on."

"I need to – " Alex doubled over, panting from the long sprint, "talk to you."

They moved into the shade of Dan's porch. "What's up? Did you see another condor?"

"No." Alex's heart was racing. He spoke between staggered gulps of air. "Josh and I took a walk . . . to the swimming hole . . . see if we could spot some animals."

Dan shook his head, "Unlikely this time of day."

"Yeah. We just . . . goofed around, sat on the bank . . .

That's when I heard it."

"Sit down; get your breath," Dan said. "You're red as a beet."

Alex plopped into a canvas chair and put his head between his knees. Dan went inside and returned with a big glass of water. Alex guzzled it down.

"Okay," Dan said, taking the empty glass. "Now, what did you hear?"

"Something falling in a tree on the slope just east of the swimming hole."

"Did it hit the ground?"

Alex shook his head. "No, that's the thing."

"Probably a squirrel."

"No," Alex insisted. "It sounded much bigger than that."

Dan thought a moment. "Maybe a dead limb came down and got tangled before it hit the ground."

"But I think I saw something. I mean, I'm sure I saw something."

"Did Josh see something, too?"

"No, he wanted to come back here. After he left I searched the three largest trees in the direction the noise came from. When I didn't see anything I started to leave, but then I heard the sneeze."

"Sneeze?"

"Yes. I was sure it came from up in the oak, so I went back and really scanned the limbs. At first I couldn't see anything and then, there they were."

"Who?"

"That's just it. I don't know. It was just a pair of eyes staring straight into mine, never blinking. It was creepy."

"Maybe it was a mountain lion. Remember, we heard

one just the other night."

"No, it wasn't any kind of cat. The eyes looked more . . . . human. Do you think it could have been a bear?"

"It's possible. I've seen evidence of bear several times, mostly pieces of honeycomb next to ground bee's holes, some footprints in the snow. But in all the time I've been here, I've only spotted one, and then it was just the back end lumbering into the forest."

"What else could it have been?"

"Maybe one of the campers was playing tricks on you."

"Hey, Alex, the burgers are ready!" Josh had raced over, leaving his post beside the grill. "Come on, or you're gonna get stuck with a hot dog."

"You'd better get over there," Dan said. "I plan to contact a friend of mine about the condor you think you saw yesterday. I'll check with some folks about any bear sightings around here, too. You can expect an e-mail in the next couple of weeks."

"Thanks."

"Bear sightings?" Josh said. "You saw a bear?"

"Yeah, right after you left, a huge, hungry one. I stood on my toes, held up my arms and growled. He ran away."

"Really?"

After the swim party the parents began to arrive. Many of them hurried their sons into air-conditioned cars and tore away, raising dust in a mad dash back to civilization; others lingered. The limousine that came to fetch Alex arrived long after the other campers were gone. A chauffeur leapt from the vehicle and hurried to open the back door. Alex leaned into the cool chamber.

"I'm sorry we're late, dear," his mother said. "This place is so hard to find."

"That's okay. Would you like to meet the head naturalist? He's really great."

Marjorie Perry extended a frail hand to draw him in. "Maybe next year, sweetheart. It's so hot, and we have such a long drive home."

**

Because he had witnessed a moving human den after Buck fell, the boy was not as surprised as he might have been to see one rolling across the far end of the meadow. The surprise came when one after another lumbered down the same path. Even more unexpected, he saw the same group of dens a short time later, going the opposite direction.

Had the two young humans he'd seen been carried away? How was he to join their pack if they were gone?

CHAPTER FOUR

Dan stood in the middle of the road to watch the last car, a ten passenger van filled with interns and counselors, make a left and disappear from sight. It was always an adjustment when he found himself completely alone at Muir Camp, but he had plenty to do, a long list that would keep him busy for months. He started up the road toward camp but decided to veer left instead and stroll through the shady forest above the meadow.

To make the smallest footprint possible, campers were encouraged to go single file on all of the trails, but the meadow path below remained wide; the flat expanse was simply too tempting. He looked down to where the path made a half circle around a thick, old elderberry. Invariably, some of the boys, after being told its fruit was used to make wine, would cluster beneath the bush, stick their noses in the fragrant blooms and pretend drunkenness.

At meadow's end, Dan headed down hill to the swimming hole. Wading in and then dunking under, he felt like steam must be sizzling off his back. Lolling in the shallows with his head propped on a smooth rock, he gazed at the sprawling live oak some twenty yards from the bank and thought about Alex's story of the mysterious sneeze and bear eyes.

**

The boy was still sitting in the cedar tree when an adult male appeared on the trail below. His teacher? . . . perhaps, but he was not ready to reveal himself. He returned to the water to retrieve Buck's offering. After eating heartily of liver and blackberries, he relaxed against the gentle contours of a granite boulder and sought communion with the only creature who had been a constant in his life from the beginning.

**

With news of Buck's disappearance, and no confirmation of a successful reintroduction, Condor had lingered near Black Oak Forest and was greatly relieved when the boy made connection. Tonight, he would see his charge one last time.

As the last vestiges of light played over the landscape, the boy sat in the nest of sticks with the second skin in his lap and waited for the unmistakable whoosh of Condor's wings. When it came, he stood and thrust the sky-colored second skin above his head. The signal stirred Condor's heart. Twelve years ago he'd responded to the same signal from atop an ancient redwood when a desperate mother urgently pushed a blue bundle up as far as her arms could reach. He had grabbed that bundle and soared away. This time, anxious for camouflage, he landed, quickly tucked his wings, and settled in close to the center of the tree.

Condor locked eyes with the boy. *So here you are, a good place. What have you seen since we parted?*

With his remembering, the boy transmitted all that had happened after he mounted Buck's back. Condor felt the boy's stomach contract when he recalled his brief observation of the young humans and the unsettling experience of losing his balance.

Condor reminded the boy of the importance of staying focused on The Plan. *There is a man who remains in Black Oak Forest after the young ones leave; he is your next teacher. His roots reach into the earth. He is aware of Source.*

Are there humans who are unaware of Source?

Yes.

How can that be?

I do not know. Perhaps you will come to understand.

The boy unfolded the second skin and offered Buck's heart to his longtime guardian. With the strength and courage of his old ally coursing through his veins, the vulture slipped off the branch and spread his wings to begin the long journey home.

CHAPTER FIVE

Dan was up at 5:00 a.m., determined to take advantage of the cool morning. He started with one of the cabins: rolling up mattresses, mopping floors, shuttering windows. When the temperature inched up over ninety degrees, he decided to take a break from grunge work and patrol one of the shady trails to check for man-made debris.

Now that the campers were gone, he didn't bother to lock the cottage door. He never worried about theft, but the idea of getting some time on a computer was quite a temptation for the campers. All electronic devices were strictly off limits; break that rule and the camper was sent home.

**

The boy lingered in the pine until the scorching heat forced him to move. On the arduous journey over the Sierra Nevada, it seemed as if his feet had wings, but now he was overcome by a weighty lethargy. Every transition he'd experienced during the past twelve years had had unexpected challenges, but there was symmetry, too. Communication through shared connection with Source smoothed the way to adaptation. Yesterday, he had gazed steadfastly into the eyes of a human, but there had been no trace of communion. The blood stained second skin lay empty at his side, a stark reminder of Buck's sacrifice. Leaving the tree, he returned to the stream to plunge the skin into the water until no trace of dirt or blood could be seen. He wrapped it around his waist, tangled the edges to hold it in place, then hiked up hill. Choosing a well-worn human path, he stepped firmly upon it.

**

Dan began his trail patrol at the recreated Native Peoples Village. He checked the bark dwellings, the sweat lodge and the round house; all were free of debris. He did spot a cracker someone had wedged between the bark and the long whips of grapevine that held the dwellings together, but he left it. Why deprive a hungry squirrel of a winter surprise?

Heading up hill, he chose a shady path that wound through several thick groupings of manzanita and stopped to marvel at the twisted, magenta branches. Flaking away a bit of curled bark, he stroked the cool smooth surface beneath and, as if patting the shoulder of an old friend, gave the branch a few hardy slaps.

Further on, the trail skirted two small grinding rocks next to a ravine. It gave Dan pause whenever he encountered the pocked granite surfaces where Native Peoples had prepared their harvest of acorns. But these particular ones always haunted him a little. Unlike the large one at the village, where holes were plentiful and deep, the depressions here were shallow and few, their beginnings likely interrupted by foreigners who wrenched the land from a people who had lived in this valley for thousands of years.

As he turned to continue down the trail, a flash of blue caught Dan's eye. Likely a plastic shopping bag, he thought, caught by the breeze coming up the ravine. If he was lucky it would catch on something before it drifted too far; he could use it to hold other trash he might find.

**

The boy quickened his pace as the trail took a steep descent toward a nearly dry creek-bed. Suspecting he might find something to eat, he veered off the path to investigate the sandy bottomed ravine. Sure enough, around the first bend, cattails thrived in a shallow pool. Anticipating a handful of tasty roots, he squatted and began to dig at the base of the plants.

**

As Dan approached the creek bed where the trail crossed the ravine, he spotted the flash of blue again. It wasn't being carried by the breeze, but was stuck to a mammal of some kind. Odd, he thought, and worth pursuing. The trick would be to catch up and get a good look without frightening the unfortunate creature. Maybe pine-pitch was the culprit, or chewing gum, another thing he'd like to ban from the camp.

Dropping into the ravine, Dan crept down the left side, repositioning rocks and twigs to ensure his every step would be silent. Fortunately, the breeze wafting up from the stream would keep the animal from detecting his scent. At the first bend, he dropped to all fours and then leaned forward just enough to get a filtered view through a small willow sprouting near the bank. There was the patch of blue all right, but it was no bag; it was a piece of fabric – and the fabric was wrapped around the waist of an adolescent boy who was nibbling on cattail roots from the shallow pool!

The kid looked so relaxed and healthy it seemed he must have survived on his own for some time and would probably run if surprised. Dan decided to return to the place where the trail intersected the ravine and wait there, perhaps even feign sleep. That way the boy would have the advantage of discovering him.

**

The boy was retracing his steps to the human path when he came face to face with a fawn. Why hadn't he heard her hooves on the stony wash? And why did she seem intent on blocking his way? He looked deep into her large brown eyes.

I am a guide.

The message was confusing, not because he didn't understand it, or welcome contact from his creature family, but because the fawn had used telepathy of human language to transmit the communication, the same method Condor used to prepare him for the meaning of human sounds. How could this be? The question went unanswered; as mysteriously as the fawn appeared, she was suddenly gone.

Unsure why this new guide had blocked him, he turned back and followed the creek-bed to its confluence with the main stream. He would wait for cover of darkness to find the human teacher's den.

CHAPTER SIX

Sonja Henderson stood at the edge of the canyon. Tall and muscular, her fair hair and light blue eyes spoke of strong Scandinavian roots. In sleeveless tee, shorts and hiking boots, she held an antenna in one hand while studying a receiving unit in the other. All of the condors she monitored wore a tracking tag on the wing, but it was P3's signal she was anxious to detect. The boy's reintroduction was P3's last assignment; she had expected him to return two days ago.

To top it off, Fawn disappeared this morning; Sonja suspected the suspense was too much for her daughter to resist. As proficient as Fawn had become in the art of *vivir en dos mundos,* it was no game. Should she be injured or, God forbid, killed while in animal form, the consequences would be – **beep, beep, beep**. The receiver interrupted Sonja's thoughts; P3 was home.

**

Dan waited on the trail for half an hour before creeping down the ravine for another look. The boy was gone. He must have followed the creek bed to the main stream. Undoubtedly, this wily creature was aware of Muir Camp's well worn paths and the location of the buildings, would know where to come if he needed help. I'll check the Internet, he thought, see if there's a match on the missing person postings.

The delay had given the sun time to ramp up to scorching. He'd been working seven days a week for three months. What was the hurry? Imagining the perfect afternoon, he decided to return to his cottage, lie down on his bed, and give Sonja Henderson a call – talk about old times, catch up on mutual friends and, he thought with amusement, get her take on condors, bear eyes and wild boys.

She picked up on the first ring.

"This is Dan Fisk. I don't know if you remember me. It's been a long time."

Sonja's response was a shock. "Of course I remember you, Dan. I've been expecting your call."

"Sure you have," he said, "what's it been, thirteen, maybe fourteen years since we've connected?"

"We've been watching you, Buddy."

We? Buddy? Dan didn't know if he should feel like a fool or take offense.

They talked for over two hours, and the conversation left Dan reeling. As far-fetched as it seemed, Sonja had named him as a major player in a scenario that had been in the making for more than a dozen years. She called it *The Plan for Essential Connection,* a strategy she had been an integral part of from the beginning.

"I was thrilled when I heard you got the job at Muir Camp," she told him. "Knowing the person who would receive the boy made it so much easier for all of us. I have to say, I was worried you might move on before he was ready for reintroduction."

Receive the boy? Reintroduction? This was hardly the relaxing conversation Dan had looked forward to – He sat up.

"It's crossed my mind more than once," Sonja continued, "that we worked together all those years ago just for this reason."

"Sonja, can you imagine how this sounds? You've got to admit what you're telling me is more than a little strange."

"Weird is actually the word you're looking for," Sonja said.

"Are you trying to drive me crazy?"

"Of course not, I'm just saying it's W-Y-R-D; that's the original spelling. Do you know the true meaning of that word?" she asked.

There was an edge to Dan's response. "Apparently not."

"It means fate, destiny," Sonja explained. "*God is alive, Magic is afoot.*"

"Those are Leonard Cohen's words, right?"

"Right; my mom was into Leonard Cohen, big time."

No response.

Sonja forged on. "I know what I'm saying sounds implausible, especially to us science types. But, Dan, those words describe what I've been experiencing for years." Silence. "Are you there?"

"I'm here." The conversation had taken an illogical turn Dan simply could not grasp. "Back up," he suggested. "Start from the beginning."

"Got time?"

Dan adjusted his pillow and laid back. "Plenty."

"Okay," Sonja began, "did you know my Mom worked for the San Diego Zoo?"

"Not that I recall," Dan said. "But I do know they had the first condor captive-breeding program. I think I remember reading there were only twenty-five condors known to exist when that program started."

"Actually, twenty-two," said Sonja. "The program has been a real success. My mom talked about it a lot, and when I was a senior in high school she asked the Avian Propagation Specialist if I could observe the work they were doing."

Sonja shared what it was like to be present when a hatchling emerged from its egg, how she'd had the privilege of helping raise the chicks. "In the beginning I thought they were ugly and, to be honest, a little creepy. But as soon as I slipped my hand into that puppet and began feeding and preening those gawky hatchlings, I was hooked."

"I saw a photo of one of those fake condor heads. Do you think the babies really believed a parent was doing the feeding?"

"It worked. They reproduce in the wild now and successfully raise their young."

"Hmmm," Dan mused, "I get the feeling the condor sighting I told you about might have been the real thing."

Sonja confirmed his suspicion. "Yes, it was P3 or, more accurately, Los Padres National Forest number 3. It's because of him I'm talking to you now."

Dan sat up again; this time, he planted his feet firmly on the floor. Sonja sounded sane, but he couldn't help but wonder if she was prone to exaggeration. One thing for sure, he needed to pay very close attention.

According to Sonja, it was during her third summer of working with condors that she had the first inkling P3 understood human speech. Late one afternoon, when she and a fellow worker were in the large enclosure with the more mature condors, she had made a comment about her new water bottle. "Check this out, it's stainless steel. My boyfriend gave it to me, even had my initials engraved on the side. I sure hope I can keep track of it." An hour later she was headed for the gate when P3 leapt to the bottom of the enclosure, picked up the bottle and tossed it toward her.

"I still have that bottle," she told Dan. "I keep it on an altar at home. That moment was really the beginning."

"Seems like a coincidence to me," Dan said.

"At first I thought so, too. We'd seen them play with water bottles before. But other things started happening."

"Example."

"The very next day, P3 swooped down and took a cap off of my head, gently, mind you, and that isn't easy for a twenty-five pound bird with a nine-foot wingspan."

Dan was impressed. "That must have been a shock."

"It was amazing. He kept it until I was ready to leave then dropped it in front of the gate. Those kinds of things happened over and over. I would glance up at him and nod, and he would look right at me with those ruby-rimmed eyes and tip his head. Sometimes he'd stare into my eyes for a long time and then, as if in a trance, he would close his and not move. In a minute or so, he'd look at me again, like he was checking to see if I was still paying attention. This went on for two summers. I asked other workers if they'd experienced anything like it, but they said no. They thought I was anthropomorphizing, you know, giving human attributes to an animal, so I just stopped talking about it."

"I'm sure the experience was incredible," Dan said, "but it doesn't exactly sound life changing."

"No, it doesn't. What was life changing was not that he seemed to be understanding me, it was when I realized I was beginning to understand him.

CHAPTER SEVEN

The meal of cattail roots had whetted the boy's appetite. When he reached the stream, he settled down next to a pool where rainbow trout glittered below the surface. Calling up the energy of Bear, he stabbed his hand into the water with lightning speed, snatched out one of the slithering creatures and quickly devoured it.

His encounter with the fawn, and his decision to return to the heron nest to wait for nightfall, broke the momentum he'd struggled to regain. Never before had he felt truly alone. Until now, he had been one of the pride, the pack, the colony, the herd, the clan. As the sun dropped below the horizon, the low lying sources of light appeared once again. Soon he would walk toward those glowing shards. What would he find there?

At full dark, the boy climbed down the tree to the dusty red earth and secured the second skin around his waist. Each step, the cricket song, the breath of moisture from the stream, even the beat of his own heart did not escape his full attention.

**

Dan tried to put a name to what he was feeling: stunned, shocked, disbelieving, scared, overwhelmed – fearful he would be completely inadequate to the task of introducing a wild boy to the human condition.

Logging onto his computer, he searched for more information and found a number of articles about the incident near Garberville, California back in 2000. The Governor had broken a campaign promise to stop the destruction of old growth redwoods, and a young couple, Holly Angle and Lyle Stone, had died trying to stop an electric company from cutting several of the ancient trees. The last article he read was an interview with the mother of Holly Angle; she had claimed there was a grandchild missing, a grandchild for whom she had crocheted a blue blanket.

"You mean the condor took the baby?" he'd asked Sonja.

"Yes. I'm telling you that's the wild boy you saw today. If P3 hadn't been there, he would have been killed, too."

"So you're saying the condor knew there was a chance the baby would be available for this … experiment?"

"Yes," Sonja replied. "The Council had been looking for a child to raise and reintroduce into the human race."

"And the condor realized there might be an opportunity to snatch the baby," Dan concluded. "Sonja, that's a pretty complicated scenario."

"It is," Sonja agreed. "You see, P3 was one of the first hatchlings. In the beginning, no one realized the condors shouldn't be comfortable around humans, that it could wreak havoc once they were reintroduced. So, even though they were fed with skillfully constructed puppets, they spent a lot of time with their caretakers, and just like any child, P3 learned to understand the language he was exposed to on a daily basis."

"Okay, I'll go with that, but how did you know he was watching the tree?"

"Animals communicate in many ways, one is what we would call telepathically or, perhaps more accurately, empathically."

"What's the difference?"

"Telepathy is communicating through means other than the senses; empathy is understanding another's situation, feeling or motive. Honestly, these words for no words are insufficient, but one might say empathy brought The Council of Creatures together, and telepathy allows them to communicate with each other."

"Like pictures?"

"Sort of, but it's more than that; there can be sounds as well. The connection is strengthened with practice. Like I said, it was that third summer working at the zoo when I realized if I quieted my mind and allowed a connection with P3's brain energy, I could receive his visualizations. I guess you could say P3 had the desire to communicate with me, that's empathy, and it fostered my curiosity to understand him. Over time, we learned to communicate telepathically."

Dan waited a moment before commenting on what Sonja had just tried to explain. "Okay," he said, "let me get this straight. You knew about The Council and The Plan. So you told P3 that Holly Angle and Lyle Stone had a baby and were living in a redwood tree that might be cut down?"

"The Council knew what was happening from the creatures living in that forest, and yes, it was one of the topics of my communication with P3."

Dan had spent his entire life in awe of nature, but he would never forget the astonishment he felt, the profound impact of what Sonja had revealed.

"Is there any other animal you communicate with?"

"No, but animals all over the world have been looking for human representatives. There may be more."

"Who else knows about this?" Dan asked.

"My mother-in-law and – "

Dan interrupted. "I didn't realize you were married."

"I'm a widow."

"Oh."

"And my daughter, she knows."

"You have a daughter?"

"Yes, she's the same age as the boy. Her name is Fawn."

Dan's mind raced; the whole thing was too fantastic. And yet, Alex *had* seen a condor and Dan *had*, with his own eyes, seen a boy eating and drinking like a wild animal. Sonja's enthusiasm and commitment was persuasive: It was destiny, a privilege, an honor, an imperative in a grand plan to bring balance back to the planet. He knew he'd left Sonja with the impression he would accept the role of teacher – but he'd never wanted to be a parent, foster or otherwise. He went over and over their conversation, Sonja's words relentlessly playing through his mind. "Dan, you were selected because you are the perfect person for this assignment and," (here he'd detected an audible sigh) "to be completely honest, you're pretty much the only person we've got. If someone else was running Muir Camp, The Council would have chosen that person. As it happens, that person is you."

How does one respond to a statement like that?

Pacing around the small cottage did nothing to diminish the intensity building in Dan's chest. He decided to go for a run. Tree roots and rocks on the hilly six-mile loop were enough of a distraction to keep him from thinking about the boy's fate. Back at the cottage, he took a shower and made himself something to eat. Normally, on an evening like this, he would leave his dirty dishes in the sink, but he took time to wash them meticulously, dry them and put them back in the cupboard. Finally, he could no longer avoid the inevitable.

The article he'd printed from the Internet sat on his desk. Photos of Holly Angle and Lyle Stone stared at him from the page. They had lived in the tree for nearly two years. How could he not do his part? After all, he was an educator, a good one. The kid is twelve years old. Sonja said she would always be available to help guide the process. How hard could it be? Little by little his resistance was dismantled, and Dan began to prepare for his guest. The boy would need clothing and a place to store it, a bed – a toothbrush for heaven's sake. He would make a drive into town this evening, go to the market and stock up. The kid could show up anytime.

Racing to the lodge, he rummaged through the lost and found, selected shorts and shirts and threw them into the washing machine. He lugged a mattress from one of the cabins to his cottage, collected bedding and a pillow. The trip into town and back took nearly three hours; he made it home just before dark. Now, there was nothing to do but wait.

The main electrical breaker for the entire camp was located in Dan's cottage, a safety precaution in case of fire. After the campers left he made a point of using the minimum power required for his simple lifestyle: pumping water into the gravity feed tank, running the washing machine, recharging his computer and cell phone. Opening the metal door to the breaker box, he pulled down on the hefty lever.

**

The boy's excellent night vision and stealthy walk were attributes developed during his year with Feline. He took a trail in the general direction of the curious low lights, leaving it briefly to investigate several irregular shapes in the forest: a large nest of grapevine and cedar bough filled with acorns, dens made of bark, an earthen cave smelling of fire and a round stone structure. Pressing on, he discovered a cluster of dens of a different kind; the low lying lights he had seen from a distance shone like tiny moons next to each one.

Further on was a den where light glowed from within. Approaching cautiously, he saw an adult male inside, the one who *stays alone after the young ones leave*. He considered making himself known, but suddenly every light source disappeared.

It would not be wise to surprise a human in the dark, better to sleep in one of the bark dens close by and meet his teacher at sunrise.

**

Dan awoke at the crack of dawn. He dressed, went to the lodge to retrieve the wet clothes from the washing machine and then hung them on the line behind the cottage.

Mother-nature would suck the moisture out of them in less than an hour. Next, he brewed coffee and started a hearty breakfast of sausage, eggs, potatoes and toast, hoping the smell would entice his guest to come out of hiding. Growing boys, no matter who or where from, were always hungry.

**

Lazily, the boy opened his eyes and was surprised to see how brilliant the sun shone on the ground outside. He stretched and stepped out of the bark den into an already warm day. Taking a few minutes to explore the environs of his sleeping place, he examined more closely the nest of acorns, the mud mound smelling of smoke, the round stone den. A large flat stone, with many deep depressions on its surface, dominated the landscape. He heard faint murmuring sounds there but could not see the source. Nearing the teacher's den, he detected an aroma as unfamiliar as the scent of the young males he'd encountered at the stream, but the smell did not irritate, or make him feel like sneezing; instead, he began to salivate.

Food?

CHAPTER EIGHT

"Mom, I *have* to go back."

Sonja did not intend to raise her voice, but before she knew it, she was slamming her cup on the kitchen counter and shouting at her daughter. "Fawn, the answer is no!"

The argument had been going on ever since Fawn returned from Muir Camp. Sonja fought to regain a calm demeanor. "You went without permission once; you are not to do it again."

"Mom," Fawn whined.

"Make no mistake, young lady; if you don't follow the rules, it will be your grandmother you have to answer to. Now go to your room and get ready for school. You don't want to be late the first day of junior high."

"But he needs me," Fawn pleaded.

Sonja put a banana into Fawn's lunch bag. "You're right," she said, "he does need you, and you will be of no help if you forge ahead on your own."

"But . . ."

"Your grandmother has made it very plain that no one

but herself, The Council and me are to know about your gift, not even Robert. The gift was given to you for a specific purpose. Robert must enter the human world on his own. The struggles he will experience with his human teacher are as important as the struggles he experienced with all of his animal mentors."

"But how will he learn human language?" Fawn countered. "Humans learn language when they're babies. You said yourself that P3 learned to understand English because he was exposed to it as soon as he came out of his shell. Robert is the same age as I am, and he's never uttered a word. He doesn't even know he has a name. I can help!"

"Fawn," Sonja began, "There is a plan and –"

Fawn didn't give Sonja a chance to finish. "Can't you hear what I'm saying? And how many times do I have to tell you, I hate bananas!" She snatched the banana out of the bag and dramatically replaced it with an apple. "Dad would have listened to me," she said under her breath.

Sonja sighed; she didn't have time for this. Why did Fawn always have to argue, have to have everything explained umpteen times? She took a deep breath, sat down at the kitchen table, then nudged the other chair with her foot. "Come on," she said. "Let's sit down for a minute."

Fawn flopped into the chair, folded her arms across her chest and dropped her head. Long, straight, black hair covered her face.

Sonja could sense her daughter was starting to cry. "Sweetheart," she said, softly. "I wish your father was here, too, but you and I both know what he would say."

Fawn was not in the mood to be babied. She came back at her mother with vengeance. "How would you know," she said. "You're just a white scientist. I'm not like you."

Buying time to calm down, Sonja grabbed her own long hair and twisted the blonde bundle into a knot. "That doesn't change the fact that your father, the Native American, and I, the white scientist, were chosen to bring you into this world." Fawn looked up. "What did you say?" She glared at her mother. "Am I just some experiment? Did you and Dad get together to produce some freak who would do your bidding?"

"Fawn, how could you –"

Fawn's pounding heart punctuated her accusations. "Did you even love each other? Were we really a family? Why do you call the boy by Dad's name, anyway?" Her frustration boiled over like a steaming cauldron. "Is Dad the father of that kid, too?" she screamed. "How sick is that!"

"Fawn!" Sonja said, sharply, "I told you all about the boy's parents. They were trying to stop –"

"I know, I know, they sat in a redwood tree . . . blah, blah, blah."

"I'm going to let that comment pass but only because I know how upset you are." Sonja lowered her volume, slowed her response. "I can assure you that your father and I were very much in love."

"Come on, Mom," Fawn said with a little less angst in her voice. "It was just part of *The Plan*, right? I bet you and Dad would never have met if it wasn't for Grandmother."

"Of course we would have. I was working there to introduce P3 and the rest of the cohort into the wild. I met a lot of Native Americans. Your Grandmother Isabelle was one of the first, and your father just happened to walk into her kitchen when I was visiting. I would have met him somewhere, eventually." She looked at her brown skinned, black eyed daughter, so like the man she had fallen in love with. "Oh, Fawn," Sonja said, "he was the first man I'd ever met that saw me for who I am. It was divine; he was my soul mate. " "I'm glad to hear that," Fawn said ... and she meant it. "But in a way you're right," Sonja admitted. "One could say it was divine providence, too." "What does that mean?" "It means something was destined to happen." A warm wave came over Sonja as she recalled those early days when she and Robert Arredondo first met. A gentle smile softened her brow; suddenly she looked younger. "Your dad and I were shocked that your grandmother approved of us spending time with each other. It's not like she planned for us to become a couple, but as soon as you were conceived, she knew you would have the gift."

Fawn's angry energy finally dissipated. "What if I don't want the gift?"

"You're the only one who can initiate transformation ... you don't ever *have* to."

"Yes I do," Fawn said. "You know I do."

Sonja took Fawn's hands in her own. "Shape-shifting is not a game, Fawn. It can be dangerous."

"Mom, I know that."

"Do you know what happened to Buck?"

"No."

"He was shot when he was taking Robert to be reintroduced."

"Are you sure? Did they find his body?"

"They found blood and entrails. I've hesitated telling you; I knew you'd be upset."

Fawn's throat constricted. "It's not fair," she moaned.

"No," Sonja agreed, "many things are not fair. We have to accept that. So you see, my girl, if you make a mistake, if you are in the wrong place at the wrong time, I could lose you."

"You're not going to lose me."

"Fawn, you must not shift without consulting Grandmother or me; do you understand?" Sonja pressed her point. "One of us has to know exactly where you will be."

"What if The Council gives me an assignment?" Fawn asked.

"They know only one side. Even P3 is very limited in his understanding of the human being. Anything The Council asks of you has to be approved by your grandmother. She is the final authority."

CHAPTER NINE
_____

Dan had almost given up. The scrambled eggs were looking pretty chewy. How long should he keep breakfast warm? Maybe the scent of sausage wasn't the bait he'd hoped for.

Oh well, a leisurely breakfast was a luxury he hadn't enjoyed since last winter; that was reason enough for cooking this morning. Scooping eggs, potatoes and the coveted sausage onto his plate, he sat at the table and tried his best to take time to enjoy every bite.

When he went to the counter to pour himself a second cup of coffee, a movement outside the kitchen window caught his eye. It seemed food had not been the attraction, but a line of clothes strung between the trees. There he was, the wild boy, examining a clothespin. After some consideration, he freed a pair of khaki shorts and put them on.

**

The scent of food, though strange, was comforting. Each new group of creatures the boy lived with shared their nourishment as a sign of acceptance. But when he spotted several second skins swinging between two trees, he realized that the human tradition of a second skin would be the first test of his ability to observe and adapt. The skin Doe had given him was the second skin of an infant; he felt sure he was being directed to replace it with an adult skin before meeting his teacher.

The skins were attached to a vine with small sticks. After scrutinizing how the sticks held the skins, he released one of them and stepped into the two holes that accommodated his legs. Several times the skin dropped to the ground until he solved the puzzle of keeping it in place by slipping a round piece through a small opening. Hands free, he discovered oriole-like nests on each side of the skin and placed his own infant skin into one of them. Confident now, he approached the opening to the den, ready to meet his teacher and share the nourishment of human food awaiting him there.

**

The two stared at each other through the filter of the screen door, both unconsciously holding their breath. The elder pushed the screen open and stepped aside. The boy crossed the threshold. They stood for a moment, making eye contact. The teacher held out one hand. When the boy mimicked the gesture, the teacher grasped the boy's hand and then shook it. "Dan" the teacher intoned, patting his chest. The boy stood firm, maintained eye contact. The teacher patted the boy's chest and made the sound, "Robert." The boy stiffened, maintained eye contact, flared his nostrils.

**

The odor of what the boy had assumed was food smelled

acrid, yet oddly enticing, signaled rot, yet stimulated his salivary glands. When he sniffed in an effort to align the scent with something familiar, the teacher broke eye contact and turned his back, giving the boy an opportunity to survey the interior of the space. Every nest, dam, den, hive, burrow, cave or hollow he'd witnessed pulsated with life, but here he sensed a profound feeling of stagnation in the plethora of lifeless matter. Though curious, he had to suppress an impulse to leave the confines of this den.

**

The boy had not moved while he was busy at the kitchen counter, but as soon as Dan sat down at the table, the boy did the same. When Dan took a bite of toast; the boy pinched a bit of egg between his fingers and put it in his mouth. A fork sat untouched next to the plate, and Dan realized he should have reserved a few potatoes for himself, eaten something that required a fork. But there was plenty of time for that – nine months to be exact, nine months until the first campers arrived, nine months until "Robert" would have to blend with his peers.

To Dan's delight, the boy ate everything. Moments later he was up and out of the cottage, losing his breakfast just outside the door. Dan walked to the window in time to see the boy sweep dirt and pine needles over the mess and then walk to a shady spot near the edge of the pool to munch on grass.

After the breakfast disaster, Dan's original trepidation made a comeback, this wasn't going to be so easy. But the boy returned to the cottage seemingly unfazed, and when

Dan offered him a glass of water, Robert's fascination at watching the cool liquid run from tap to vessel, overrode Dan's doubt. Like a parent on Christmas morning, he found himself wanting to surprise and delight the boy. Sitting in the old lounge chair in the corner, he raised and lowered the foot rest; then he stood and waited for Robert's reaction. The boy immediately sat in the chair and proceeded to work the lever over and over again until Dan finally coaxed him outside to tour some of the other buildings.

At the lodge, Dan began reciting the same orientation lecture he had given for eight years. "This stone fireplace," he said, slapping the river stones that rose from floor to vaulted ceiling, "was the original fireplace of the home of the woman who donated the four hundred acres that is now John Muir Environmental Camp." The boy watched Dan's mouth intently, ears tipping slightly this way and that, as he received the cacophony of sound. When Dan patted the river stones, he did the same.

With Robert at his heels, Dan pushed through the swinging door that led to the kitchen. When the door swung back and smacked the boy in the face, Dan placed the boy at a safe distance and then pushed the door hard to display how it swung in both directions. Robert began testing the reaction of the door depending on the strength of his own push. Like the lever on the lounge chair, the activity seemed to be endlessly entertaining.

"That's enough," Dan said, but the boy didn't stop. Dan grabbed the door, held it still, and looked into Robert's wide eyes. "That's enough," he said firmly.

The boy attempted to emulate the sound.

Dan held up a flat hand, Robert did the same. "Enough,"

Dan repeated.

"Enough," said Robert with surprising clarity.

Not surprisingly, the huge commercial kitchen soon became a playground. Dan would turn a faucet, Robert would turn the faucet. Dan would squirt a nozzle, Robert would squirt a nozzle. Dan opened the door of one of the refrigerators, stuck his hand inside, touched the boy's cheek and said, "Cold."

"Cold," the boy mimicked, then attempted to climb inside.

When Dan noticed Robert eyeing the faucets and nozzles, he knew the kid wanted to return to the dishwashing area. Why not? But, unlike the first time, Robert's grasp on the nozzle was not tentative, and the kitchen got a quick hosing down. Dan held up his hand and shouted, "Enough!" When Robert dropped the nozzle it instantly shut off, but the mix of panic and dismay on the boy's face told Dan it was time to get outside.

Dan packed dried fruit, nuts, and water, and the two of them set out to explore the miles of trails crisscrossing Muir Camp. Now it was Dan's turn to be amazed. At the slightest noise, Robert would scurry up a tree at lightning speed, become invisible and moments later appear at Dan's side. When they reached the stream, Robert took off his shorts and plunged in. Dan sat on the bank munching the snacks and drinking bottled water while the boy pulled claws off of a crawdad, sucked out the meat and drank from the stream.

It was late afternoon when they returned from the hike. Robert sat down next to a granite boulder near the cottage, leaned heavily against the rough, sparkling surface and closed his eyes. Dan went inside to check his e-mail and scan the Internet. When he finally looked up from the computer, the boy was gone.

**

After he and his teacher returned from the stream, the boy rested against a warm boulder and fell into a deep sleep. He awoke from a nightmare where water shot from his fingers rendering them useless, where his new earth colored second skin was soaked in Buck's steamy blood, where his every attempt to take nourishment was followed by uncontrollable retching. 'Enough, Enough, Enough,' thundered in his head. Trying to expel the disturbing imprint of the dream, he shook his head vigorously . . .

Confusion.

Where was his creature family? With the exception of the brief encounter with a fawn yesterday, he'd been left completely alone. His heart was racing, and he did what came naturally – he ran. He ran and did not stop until he reached the pine and climbed to the nest of the the great blue heron, Water gushed from his eyes; he trembled uncontrollably. In a desperate attempt to summon his friend, he held his sky-blue skin aloft ... *Come, Condor, come.*

CHAPTER TEN

Tired after a long day in the field, Sonja made dinner while Fawn sat at the kitchen table grumbling about how homework was invading her life. The phone rang just as Sonja was about to drain the pasta. "Get that, will you, Fawn?"

Fawn rolled her eyes and picked up the receiver. When a male voice asked for her mother, she tried to hand the phone to Sonja.

"Put it on speaker and set it on the window sill." – Another roll of the eyes. Sonja leaned toward her daughter and lowered her voice. "And cool it with the face crimes."

Fawn pushed the orange speaker button, set the phone on the sill over the kitchen sink and returned to the table. Slouching over an algebra paper, she let out another groan.

Sonja spoke in the direction of the receiver. "Hello."

"Sonja, this is Dan. He's gone."

The steam from the draining pasta rose up in a warm fog around Sonja's face. "So, he did show up."

"This morning."

"When did you last see him?"

"A few hours ago. We took a long walk. When we got back he sat down, leaned against a boulder in front of the cottage and closed his eyes. I decided it would be a good time to catch up on my e-mail and, well, you know how time flies when you're on the computer. I feel terrible for ignoring him. I checked on him once; he seemed to be sleeping. The next time I looked, he was gone."

"Don't worry, he'll be back."

"Sonja, are you sure I'm the right . . ."

She didn't give Dan a chance to finish. "Tell me how you finally met."

Fawn cocked an ear toward the conversation. She couldn't believe her luck; she was getting a first-hand account of Robert's reintroduction.

Dan launched into telling Sonja all that had happened since they'd last talked. "Right after we hung up yesterday, I started getting ready. I dug through some clothes in the lost-and-found and threw them in the washer. Early this morning I hung them on a line near the cabin, and then I cooked up a big breakfast thinking the smell might entice him to come.

"About eight o'clock, I spotted him out at the clothes-line. He was obviously intrigued with the clothespins and the shirts and shorts hanging there. He finally chose a pair of khaki shorts and put them on, even figured out the button. Next thing you know, we were face to face at my screen door. It was intense just standing there, staring at each other. I'll tell you one thing; he's much more comfortable with eye contact than I am."

Swirling bits of garlic and olive oil into the pasta, Sonja

asked, "Did he eat the breakfast?"

"Yep, scarfed it down and threw it up just as fast."

Fawn made a gagging noise. Sonja shook her head at her daughter and put a finger to her lips.

"Well, there's your first lesson," Sonja said, as she set the salad on the table. "Changing the diet of a wild creature is a risk. How much do you know about wild edible foods?"

"Some, but I've never tried to survive on them. Do you think he can adapt to what I eat?"

Fawn pointed at the salad repeatedly.

Sonja nodded her head. "Of course, but you'll have to pay close attention to the order you introduce things. Raw greens should be okay."

"I wish I'd thought of that. He ate grass right after he lost his breakfast."

"Like a sick cat," Sonja said.

"You know what's really amazing?" Dan continued. "He sucks meat from crawdad claws, drinks by kneeling at a stream that could easily have giardia in it and looks healthy as a horse. Doesn't say much for my cooking."

"His body has adapted to the diets of his teachers. Apparently, he's immune to giardia."

Dan's excitement came over the speaker loud and clear. "You wouldn't believe how quickly he perceives how things work. When I showed him the lodge kitchen, he figured out knobs and nozzles right away." Dan chuckled. "Actually, he gave the kitchen quite a hose down. That's when I decided we'd end the lodge tour and take a hike. His dexterity and strength are unbelievable. The kid scurries up trees and boulders like a squirrel."

To Sonja, it sounded like Dan was moving a little too

fast, but criticism at this stage would be a mistake. She could tell he was already starting to bond.

"Guess the first word he pronounced," said Dan.

"Robert," Sonja replied, confidently.

"Nope."

"You remembered to call him that, right?"

"Yes, I remembered, but I don't think he understood that to be his name."

"Well then, it must have been 'Dan'."

"Nope."

"I give."

"Enough."

"Enough?"

"Yes, complete with a flat palm hand signal."

Sonja laughed. "That makes sense. You have a brilliant toddler on your hands. Two year olds hear 'no' all the time; Enough – nice variation." Sonja set a block of Parmesan cheese and the grater in front of Fawn.

"You understand," Dan said.

"Of course I do. I've raised teenagers with nine-foot wing spans, keeps you on your toes."

Fawn cringed at the description of Robert as an over-grown toddler. This Dan guy sounded like a big kid describing a new pet. What did they think it was like for Robert? Where was the respect for a boy who survived a childhood of being bounced from one environment to another?

As her mother reassured the head guy at Muir Camp he was right for the job, Fawn picked up her algebra book, went to her room and focused on her homework. She had to get to bed early. Like it or not, there were things she needed to attend to after nightfall.

Following dinner and dishes, Fawn took a shower and got ready for bed. Standing in the hallway, she glanced into her mother's room. "See you in the morning."

"Going to bed? It's only eight o'clock."

"I didn't sleep that well last night."

"Did you finish your homework?"

Fawn yawned and then smiled. "All done."

Sonja was relieved. Fawn's attitude seemed to have softened. "Come in here a second," she said. "I need a hug." They didn't hug often these days. It felt so good to wrap her arms around her daughter. Stepping back, she held Fawn at arm's length and grinned. "Aren't those pink and yellow pajamas just crazy? What was I thinking?"

"I like them," Fawn said. "They're really comfortable."

Sonja thought Fawn's faced looked a little flushed. "Are you feeling all right?"

"Mom, I'm fine." Fawn took another lengthy yawn. "See you in the morning."

Thankful her squeaky closet door was ajar, Fawn slipped inside to retrieve an old wooden box from a shelf at the back. What was contained within would not have tempted a thief. A child untarnished by modern amusements, however, would see each item as unique, worthy of examination: a raven-black rock smooth as glass, a geode unbroken, a human tooth, the tooth of a deer, a wild turkey feather and a leather pouch smelling of ephedra and sage. *Just this one more time,* she thought; she was doing the right thing – the thing, after all, she had been born to do.

Sitting at the edge of her bed with the box on her lap,

Fawn visualized her intent, selected each item, held it in her palm until she sensed its pulse and then returned it to the box. One by one, the energy of the sacred objects infused her being. Lastly, she removed the pouch, inhaled the scent and quietly repeated the chant of her fore-mothers. A feathery tingling in her chest radiated out through her arms and legs, followed by a sensation of complete weightlessness. Like being swept away by a slow-motion tornado, she was gently jostled to and fro and then, just as gently, was released from its grip. When she opened her eyes she looked down not at feet but at delicate hooves standing in the duff at the base of a ponderosa pine.

**

Sonja was having a hard time getting to sleep. She wasn't worried – well, not exactly. Robert would return to Dan's cabin, of that she was sure, but Fawn's reaction to the phone call gnawed at her conscience. In trying to empathize with Dan, she must have seemed insensitive to Robert's situation. Stomping out of the kitchen was a clear indication that Fawn was upset; she seemed okay before she went to bed though.

Had Robert been reintroduced a hundred years ago, the adjustment would have been so much easier. Even in the remote setting of Muir Camp, technology was part of everyday life. Sonja was contemplating how Robert might react to a city when she heard tapping at her window and looked up to see P3 just outside. Pulling on a robe, she joined him in the back yard. Behind the ever-present wisdom in the great vulture's ruby-rimmed eyes, she saw concern.

The boy had tried to contact P3 again, but the vibration

was distorted. Red-tail hawk reported the boy had returned to the heron nest. The concern was not for his safety, but that his ability to enter the sacred space of psychic communication had been compromised.

To enter the realm of exchange, P3 explained, *one must be confident, free of anxiety. Deep calm is essential for communion.*

Sonja's heart skipped a beat. Maybe there was more to her sleeplessness than Fawn's reaction to her conversation with Dan. She took a conscious breath and sought clarity in the channel between P3 and herself.

When I tapped at your window, you felt no anxiety. Why?

"Because you are familiar, I feel safe when I see you."

The boy does not feel safe.

"But surely there have been other times he was afraid."

He is not afraid; fear is a reaction to thought. The boy's awareness and competence does not come from thought.

"He must be so confused."

Yes, and we knew it would be so.

"I will speak to his teacher."

When Dan asked Sonja to explain how she and P3 communicated, she had used the word telepathy, knowing full well the word was inadequate. The language barrier seemed to be language itself. She needed to call Dan before going to sleep, needed to clarify some concepts she hadn't understood clearly until now.

**

After Sonja's call, Dan realized that what he had assumed would be exciting, or even desirable to the boy, was likely upsetting and impossibly strange. Sonja had told him of Fawn's reaction when she overheard their conversation.

"I only know how to be one kind of teacher," Dan told her. "Obviously, I lack the kind of expertise required for this assignment."

"I made a mistake using the word teacher," Sonja said. "This situation doesn't call for expertise, it calls for authenticity ... and that's much more subtle, much more difficult. It is our job to show him how to adapt, but in actuality, he is *our* teacher. We mustn't forget that."

"I thought I was supposed to get him ready to fit in with the boys at camp by next summer," Dan reminded her.

"He's quick," Sonja replied, "He'll learn a whole lot by observation."

"I have to set limits. Remember what happened with the nozzle in the kitchen."

"Of course you have to set limits, but you also have to pay attention to what you encourage."

"Touché," Dan said. "I see what you're saying."

"I'm learning the same lesson with Fawn," Sonja said. "Transition isn't easy for any of us. The most important thing we can do is stay alert, not be sidetracked by the velvet rut."

Dan thought about that. "You're right. I can't believe I automatically gave him my same old orientation speech. He's going to keep me on my toes. I hesitate to say thank you but..."

"But?"

"Thank you."

**

Fawn nestled down at the base of the pine to wait. The boy needed her now; getting permission would have taken too long. Grandmother's voice niggled at the edge of her awareness but this, she assured herself, would be the last time she shifted without consent. She curved her long neck into her chest and closed her eyes – good to catch a bit of sleep while she had the chance. She did, after all, need to be up and ready for school early tomorrow.

**

The boy's call to Condor went unanswered. He knew he must return to his human teacher. As he lowered himself from branch to branch, his natural lithe step was impeded by trembling legs. To his surprise, the fawn he'd seen in the ravine the day before was curled at the base of the tree. She lifted her head; her large, brown eyes conveyed soothing acceptance and the blessed gift of animal companionship. She followed him to the bark den he had slept in the night before and, spooned together, they drifted into a deep, comforting sleep.

CHAPTER 11

Her first awareness was the smell of packed clay and then the gentle pressure of breath in, breath out from the warm body at her back. When Fawn finally opened her eyes, a jolt ran from the bottom of her hooves to the top of her – Hooves! *Oh no, I'm supposed to be at school!* The intensity of that thought propelled her out of a warm coat of spotted fur and plopped her down on the tile floor of Mr. Fanucchi's classroom at Los Portales Middle School. She looked at the clock above the teacher's desk, 7:45, and heard a key unlocking the classroom door.

"Fawn! What are you doing in here?"

"Uh ... I got locked in yesterday afternoon?"

"I don't think so. Are those pajamas you're wearing?"

"I must have been sleep-walking."

"I don't know how you got in here, but I think you might want to go to the office, call home, and have someone bring appropriate clothing for you to wear today."

"Good idea. Are there any kids outside?"

"Quite a few, actually."

Fawn took a fortifying breath and bolted for the door. As she streaked past a group in the hallway she shouted, "Been rehearsing for a play. Gotta change."

"What play?" someone snickered as she whizzed by, "Clowns-R-Us?"

She made it to the office with a modicum of harassment. "Can I call my mom?"

"You must be Fawn," the secretary said. "You're Mom called a few minutes ago, wondering if you were here. That's quite an outfit you've got there."

"I thought I'd wear them just for fun, but after I got to school I realized it wasn't such a good idea."

"Use the phone at my desk; just dial nine first."

"Thanks … Mom?"

"Are you at school?"

"Yes."

"Wait in the teacher's parking lot."

Fawn hunkered down in the far corner of the lot to avoid the students arriving by bus. In one way it seemed to take forever for her mom to arrive, in another, her dread made the sight of her mom's car turning into the lot come way too soon. "I'm sorry," she said as soon as she slipped into the seat.

Sonja was silent. Instead of turning right out of the lot as Fawn expected, they turned left, and when Sonja turned onto the freeway ramp heading west, she realized they weren't going home.

The silent treatment lasted for almost an hour before Sonja reached into the back seat and handed Fawn a brown paper bag. "Eat," she ordered.

Fawn settled the bag on her lap. When she unrolled the top she expected to see a hand of bananas (her least favorite food on the planet,) but when she peered inside, she saw all of her favorites: strawberry yogurt, sesame seed bagel with hummus and cucumber, and a coconut milk. A peace offering didn't make sense. She had, after all, broken the rule, but the message seemed to be, I understand, and Fawn was grateful. "I promise," she began, "I'll never…"

"Never say never, Fawn," Sonja said. "Life isn't like that. You went, you're back, and I am, obviously, not the person to impress upon you the importance of letting someone know your intentions."

"Grandmother?"

Sonja's voice was calm and firm. "Yes, it's best you live with her now."

When they reached a gate, a few hundred feet beyond the paved road, Sonja stopped the car and turned off the engine.

"I'll get the gate," Fawn said.

"No need, this is as far as I go."

"What?"

"Your pack is in the back seat."

"I'm walking? Mom, it's twelve miles."

"You have plenty of time before dark," Sonja said. "You might want to take off your shoes; your dad always did that, walked in barefoot. He felt it was important to have contact with the land."

Sonja gazed through the windshield at the rutted track beyond the gate. "You can follow the road or you can use the path on the right. It ends just above Isabelle's house."

Fawn was stunned. She hesitated a moment before

getting out of the car thinking, surely, Sonja would say more. But the steely silence was not broken and, after retrieving her backpack and closing the door, she watched her mother turn the car around and drive away.

**

The boy had slept soundly until the warmth at his back suddenly disappeared. He rolled into the slight depression where the fawn had been lying and felt the absence of her calming companionship . . .

Missing.

He focused on specks of dust floating in a slender thread of sunlight inside the bark den. Never before had he left a teacher after a transition; never had a transition been so jolting. Condor conveyed his experience of reintroduction as a long awaited return to his natural way of being, fully in harmony with Source. But from the first moment the boy encountered his own kind, his senses were assaulted by forces so foreign, he felt only loss of connection.

He returned to the stream to satisfy his hunger with watercress and trout and was observing a spider creating the anchoring lines for a web when he heard a two legged creature approach. From the opposite bank, the teacher raised his hand in greeting; the boy waded through deep water to join him on the other side.

He followed his teacher down the length of the meadow path to the trail of the moving dens. He knelt to study the wide, scarred swath, noting the long, deep depressions in the dense layer of broken rock.

"Tire tracks." It was the first time his teacher had made a sound since they left the stream. The boy stared at the teacher's mouth.

"Tire," his teacher said again.

The boy tried, "Tire."

"Tracks," said the teacher.

He attempted the second sound, "Tracks."

"Tire tracks," his teacher said.

"Tire tracks," mimicked the boy. The teacher bobbed his head up and down, showed his teeth.

**

Dan led Robert to the parking area next to the barn where the earth was bare and dusty. He pointed to the pattern left by his thick-soled sandals and said, "Dan's tracks." Then he indicated the barefoot prints near his own and said, "Robert's tracks." Next he opened the double doors of the barn to reveal his old pickup. "Tire," he said, pointing to the wheel.

Robert touched the hard black surface, ran his fingers across the grooved pattern.

"Tire," Dan repeated.

"Tire," said Robert.

Dan looked into Robert's eyes. "Tire tracks," he said, hoping to see recognition in the boy's expression.

"Tire tracks," said Robert. The boy displayed his teeth, moved his head up and down, attempting a facsimile of Dan's smile and nod.

Dan rushed outside. "Dan," he said, pointing to his own chest and again to the prints his sandals had made. "Dan's tracks."

"Dan's tracks," Robert repeated.

Dan could hardly contain himself. He pointed to Robert's chest. "Robert," he said, his voice rising with enthusiasm.

The boy pointed to his own barefoot prints and said, "Robert's tracks."

He gets it! Dan slapped the kid on the back like a player congratulating a teammate – Like a startled deer, the boy lurched to the side and sprinted toward the forest.

"Robert," Dan shouted. The boy slowed, stopped, and turned toward his teacher. Dan held up his hand.

Duplicating the hand gesture, the boy said, "Enough."

"Enough," said Dan.

CHAPTER 12

Fawn loosened the tie at the top of her backpack and looked inside. On top was a pair of jeans, a tee shirt, underwear, and a large, red handkerchief rolled together with a canvas sun hat. She looked up and down the road, confirmed that she was, indeed, completely alone, and changed her clothes. She felt the shape of her boots in the bottom of the pack, but for now, like her father, she would walk barefoot.

Heaving the pack onto her back, Fawn buckled the waist belt, then automatically checked the side pockets for water containers; both pockets held full, one liter bottles. She pulled out the one on the right side and was shocked to see she was holding the very bottle that had occupied a special place on her mother's alter for as long as she could remember – the bottle that symbolized P3's first attempt at communication. It was one of Sonja's greatest treasures. Tears welled up; she wiped her eyes with the handkerchief and then tied it around her neck. She still trusts me, Fawn thought; I will never betray her

trust again – and like an echo, she heard her mother's voice
. . . *Never say never, Fawn; life isn't like that.*

After a few steps, Fawn began calculating how long it
would take her to reach Grandmother's house. She was sure
of the mileage; they had clocked it on the odometer years
ago. Even in a car, those twelve miles took a long time; the
rutted road had lots of switchbacks near the end. Surely, the
path would be more direct. *I generally walk close to three
miles an hour, but on the flat part I might do more. The hills
could slow me down a little, but Mom's right; I can easily
get there before dark.*

Once she set a good, steady pace, Fawn began to feel
exhilarated, strong, independent. The sun was straight overhead by the time she reached the place where the trail turned
uphill, and she decided to take a break in the shade of one of
the few trees in sight. She searched her pack, hoping her
mother had stuck in a piece of fruit. She smelled it before
she saw it – a disgusting, brown-spotted banana. Her first
impulse was to be angry, but she was way too hot for anger.
She buried the thing, then drank the rest of the water from
the coveted old bottle. When she was young, her mother
would allow her to touch the bottle but had made it clear she
was never to take it from the altar – The bottle, the banana .
. . . what was her mother telling her now?

Contemplating the climb ahead, Fawn put on her
boots. A few hundred feet, and the wisdom of her decision
was confirmed. Apparently, this part of the trail had not
been used for some time. The plants that grew with last
spring's rain had not been trampled; dry, stickery vegeta-
tion covered much of the path. As the view of the road

below disappeared, the trail ahead became less clear. She ignored the flutter of her heart, gave gratitude for her boots and tramped on.

Up, always up. Each time she thought she was about to crest the hill, another rise would appear. Her shadow was lengthening; how much time had passed? More than once she thought about the contents of the old wooden box and the ancient pouch, wishing she could run sure-footed on four legs. As the afternoon wore on, she had to fight the impulse to stop, to collapse onto the ground and sob, but a force akin to a firm palm at her back, nudged her on . . . *you are part of this place, you are not in danger. Trust.*

Seven hours after setting out, Fawn stood on a ridge overlooking a verdant valley, her Grandmother's house a quick descent away. When she neared the screen on the open kitchen door she smelled the scent of fresh baked bread. Shucking her pack, she removed the red handkerchief from around her neck, wiped her face and stepped inside ... Home.

Isabelle's back was to the door. She was standing at the kitchen counter, methodically washing dishes while humming an old, familiar tune. Scrub, dip, place in drainer, scrub, dip, place in drainer. The rhythmic sound of chores at Grandmother's house had been like a heartbeat to Fawn, a welcome constant in the tumult of her early childhood. She stood in silence, admiring the thick braids running down Grandmother's back and recalled those Saturday mornings when Isabelle sat on a kitchen chair in the back yard and allowed her to brush the waist length tresses as they dried in the breeze. Gathering hair from the brush, Fawn would cast it to the wind; she found many a bird's nest with that long, dark hair swirled in its center. The black thread used to bind the ends of each braid was in sharp contrast to the snowy hair now.

Deep in reverie, Fawn was startled, but not truly surprised when, without turning around, Grandmother said, "Help me empty these pans will you, dear?" Fawn chuckled to herself, remembering how Grandmother used to say, "I've got eyes in the back of my head."

Hurrying to the counter, she picked up the pan of soapy water, and the two carried the pans outside to empty them onto the thirsty ground.

"Take your things to your room and wash up." Grandmother said. "Let's have a bit of supper then we'll talk."

When Fawn returned to the kitchen, two steaming bowls of soup and a plate of dark bread sat on the table. Grandmother had taken off her apron and pinned her braids in a large circle around the back of her head. As was the custom in this home, they ate slowly and in silence. The soup was delicious, the bread hearty. When they were finished, Fawn cleared the table while Grandmother set the teakettle on the stove.

"You don't seem surprised to see me," Fawn said.

"A friend of mine spotted you on the trail."

It unsettled Fawn to think someone had been watching her. "What friend? I didn't see anyone."

"Flicker," Grandmother replied. "He always lets me know when company is coming."

The kettle began to sing; Isabelle got up to prepare tea. When she returned to the table she set the tray between them. "Now," she said, searching Fawn's eyes, "what brings you to my door step?"

Fawn looked down. A sizable lump had formed in her throat; it took a few moments for her to respond. "Mom sort of kicked me out," she said quietly.

Isabelle poured the tea, and the two held their mugs for a moment, each contemplating the impending conversation. "Tell me more," Grandmother said.

In absence of reprimand, the lump in Fawn's throat began to dissolve. She forced herself to resume eye contact, a sign of respect and honesty. "Mom told me the next time I broke the rules, I'd have to answer to you."

"Shape shifting?" Grandmother asked.

Fawn nodded.

"Trans-location?"

"Yes . . . I mean both . . . twice."

Grandmother said nothing.

"Do you know about the boy?" Fawn asked. "The one they call Robert? After my dad, I guess."

"I do. How many years has that been?"

"Twelve. He and I were born the same year."

"Ah, yes. So, he's been reintroduced by now."

"Just a few days ago."

"Did it go smoothly?"

"No."

"Is the boy safe?"

"That's the reason I did it." Fawn's voice rose with each urgent impulse: "He needed me! It's awful! No one understands!"

"No one understands?"

"They don't know how scared he is."

"Are you sure he's scared?"

"He must be. The buck that was to deliver him to the

place of reintroduction was shot before they reached their destination. The first human food he ate made him throw up."

"Difficult," Grandmother agreed.

"And," Fawn said, "they're treating him like a baby!"

"Who's treating him like a baby?"

Fawn sat on the edge of her chair, heart pounding. "Mom and this Dan guy, the one who's supposed to be his human teacher. They totally don't get it."

"Relax, dear," Grandmother advised. "Just breathe. Robert will be fine. Transition is hard. It hurts, sometimes a little, sometimes a lot. It rubs at our edges, scrapes off some parts, stimulates new growth."

The wisdom of Isabelle's words soothed Fawn's anxious heart. She sat back, inhaled deeply and closed her eyes for a few moments. Feeling much calmer, she savored a sip of tea and took a careful look around her grandmother's kitchen. Would she be doing her homework at this table now? And for how long? No radio, no phone, no Internet.

Grandmother's cheerful voice interrupted her thoughts. "Now," she said, "let's have a piece of pie."

Settling in to her sparsely furnished room, Fawn appraised the telltale signs of her much younger self. At the end of the twin bed sat a small metal box filled with rocks, the largest the size of a man's fist, the smallest a tiny smooth pebble. Their colors seemed dull compared to the deep hues that caught her attention when they gleamed at the bottom of a shallow stream. Next to the box was one of Grandmother's baskets filled with shells she'd collected on family outings to the coast. Her treasured sticks, each one smoothed and grouped according to size, were rolled into a piece of deer hide bound with beaded string. On a rough hewn bench in the corner sat a small section of cottonwood limb, its deep hollow still protecting a dozen feathers. These were her childhood toys. Her imagining had fashioned them into villages where the people worked and played and slept and ate and danced and sang and loved each other. Slipping into her nightgown, she snuggled under the blankets. Her body was tired, but her heart was lighter than it had been for a long time.

The next morning Fawn wandered into the kitchen anticipating a warm hug, but the kitchen was empty. Through the back door she could see Isabelle, bent over, tending the vegetable garden. She called through the screen, but Grandmother did not answer. A note on the table caught her eye.

Fawn,

For these first few days we will work side by side without speaking. Pay attention to see how you can help. If need be, I will write a note to you. Much wisdom comes with silence.

Breakfast at 9:00. Please prepare a pot of mint tea.

Fawn glanced at the clock, a quarter to nine. She grabbed a pair of kitchen shears and then walked out the front door to a patch of mint growing near the rain barrel. She nipped a few fragrant stalks, returned to the kitchen, bruised the mint before stuffing it in the teapot, and set the kettle to boil. Scurrying to her room, she made her bed, dressed, combed her hair and was back in the kitchen just as the kettle started to sing.

Isabelle came through the door with a smile. After washing her hands, she put on an apron and began slicing bread from the dinner loaf. Fawn touched her on the arm and, with a questioning look, flapped her own like a hen. Isabelle nodded and handed her a wire basket. This was going to be fun, like a game of charades.

Fawn slipped through the gate of the chicken yard, swooshing at the flock gathered 'round her feet. Ducking under the low door of the hen house, she retrieved four eggs then made her escape. The kitchen was filled with the delicious scent of melting butter; while Grandmother toasted bread in a big iron skillet, Fawn made a vegetable scramble.

Morning chores came next: Fawn transferred chicken feed into a metal can, replaced the box straw and removed empty wasp nests from several of the outbuildings. Around eleven o'clock she began to think about school. She'd be in math class right now. Did anyone notice she was gone? She was daydreaming about wandering through the halls, imagining the faces of the kids she knew, until she felt a light pressure on her back and turned to see Grandmother wearing boots and holding a small tote bag. Apparently, they were going to for hike.

Little Hawk Hill rose six hundred feet to the west of Grandmother's house. The path was as familiar to Fawn as her own name. Sonja liked to tell the story of Fawn's third birthday, how she had marched up the hill chanting, "Fawn thinks she can, Fawn thinks she can." She heard those words in her mind now and grinned at the idea of her much younger self, a confident self with an uncomplicated life – before her father died.

CHAPTER 13

Dan had resisted contacting Sonja, and she had resisted in-terrupting whatever might be going on at Muir Camp. It had been a month; it was Dan who finally made the call.

"It's about time," Sonja said when she heard his voice.

"How's it going?"

"Really well."

"Great. Since I hadn't heard anything, I figured as much."

"Remember when you said it's our job to show him how to adapt, but in truth, *he* is *our* teacher?"

"I do," Sonja said.

"You used the word authenticity during that discussion. I've thought a lot about that, even looked it up."

"Ah, one of those."

"Yes, especially lately. Language is a tricky business to pass on. Want to hear what the Oxford Dictionary has to say?"

"Absolutely."

"Authenticity – of undisputed origin – genuine. It's a perfect description of Robert."

"And an infant," Sonja said, "or an animal. I look forward to meeting him. I've only seen him through P3's eyes. Tell me more."

Dan relayed the story of the first linguistic breakthrough, the *Track Event* as he called it. "It all started on the road," he explained. "Tire tracks in gravel."

Once Robert understood the concept of a name for everything, he learned so many words so quickly that, in conjunction with his natural inclination to observe and imitate, Dan was now able to assign chores the boy could complete on his own. He told Sonja how he'd set Robert to organizing the barn. With the simple example of gathering a few screws together, Robert began to line up similar items like a pack rat. Every flat surface was completely covered; each nut, bolt, washer and nail, can, plastic bottle, spoke and tube sat in its place beside another. When Dan saw what Robert had done, he led him to the kitchen where they gathered spare jars and boxes. Returning to the barn, Dan swept the small screw group into his hand and dropped them into one of the jars. That's all it took; Robert busied himself for the rest of the day with the task of containing.

"I've taken your advice," he told Sonja. "I've kept an open door, but he doesn't enter the cottage much. Remember when he first came, how he wanted to manipulate every gadget or swinging door? He's not like that now."

"More cautious?"

Dan thought for a moment. "I'm not sure if that's what it is. I never thought I would welcome some of that toddler enthusiasm again. At least he seemed to be having fun. He attempts to copy what my face looks like when I smile, sort of bares his teeth, but I don't sense a feeling of happiness or friendliness when he does it."

"Does he seem angry?"

"Not really. He's just watching. I wish we could actually connect."

"Just as it takes time to learn a verbal language, it takes time to learn a non-verbal one," Sonja said.

"The first time he put two words together I got so excited. I felt like we'd scored, you know?"

"I can imagine," Sonja said. "That's a real milestone."

"It was, and without thinking, I slapped him playfully on the back."

"I bet that got a reaction."

"Yep, he bolted and ran."

"Did he leave again?" Sonja asked.

"Nope. He stopped, held up his hand and said, 'Enough'."

Hearing the enthusiasm in Dan's voice was sobering for Sonja. Without a thought, she had bumped this good man's well-crafted life off kilter. He sounded like a proud parent. He cared now and, as she well knew, caring could open the door to despair … And Robert … he must be so lonely. Where did he sleep? Did he find solace at night? That's what Fawn had been so driven to provide. Loneliness, it had haunted Sonja for years, could wrap its tentacles around her, even in a crowd.

**

On the eighth day, Fawn awoke convinced the period of silence would be over. Surely, a whole week was enough. It had been somewhat difficult, but not so bad, really. After all, she was an only child; she knew how to entertain herself. And she liked chores – most of the time.

She and Grandmother had tended the garden, washed all the windows, patched the hen house roof. They cleared the culvert where the road crossed the creek, sanded and oiled the outdoor table and benches and hiked to the top of Little Hawk Hill to scrub the inside of the gravity-feed water tank. She spent time in her room sorting through her old things, sometimes arranging them in still life to draw in her sketch book. But today she was confident she would be greeted in the kitchen by a cheerful "Good Morning." She dressed, combed her hair, made her bed and, seeing her sketchbook on the side table, picked it up to share her drawings.

Hope was dashed as soon as she opened her bedroom door. A note was on the hallway floor, weighted with a piece of obsidian.

Dear Fawn,

The fruits of Silence are many: self-control, patience, dignity, reverence, courage.

We will continue this practice until the full moon.

Think on these things, I will return at dusk.

A dam burst. Fawn screamed, ripped the note to shreds, crumpled it into a ball and threw it down the hallway. Stomping through the empty rooms, she began to shout at the top of her lungs. "I want to go to school. I'll do algebra. I don't care if kids make fun of me, fine, I'm twelve!"

In the kitchen, she flung open a cupboard and stared at

the contents: nuts, seeds, dehydrated fruit. She wanted cereal from a box, milk from a carton. She just wanted breakfast; she didn't want to *prepare* it. And she wanted it **NOW!**

Slamming the cupboard door, Fawn bolted into the yard ready to run, but a shock of no less impact than the calamitous note, hit her right between the eyes. She was face to face with a full-grown condor.

Perched on a chair only feet from the back door, the vulture's red-rimmed eyes focused directly on her. Fawn didn't move, it didn't move. Her mind emptied, her body went rigid. It wasn't until she began to swoon from lack of oxygen that she realized she'd stopped breathing. When she did inhale, the torrent of smells was overwhelming: mint and marjoram, corn silk, tomato vine, compost and calendula, the earthy animal smell of the huge bird in front of her. Then color, unbelievably vibrant: the rich caramel brown of the hills, orange lichen blooming on rough gray boulders, green of every hue in bushes and trees, the lush vegetable garden with its deep purple eggplant, burgundy tomatoes, yellow squash, orange pumpkin, infinite shades and textures – pulsing, alive.

**

The full moon bathed the boy in gentle light and cast shadows on the ground below. Sleeping was becoming increasingly difficult. So much had happened since the last full moon, that night when he'd first sought safety in the heron nest. Now, a constant repetition of words ran through his head, an unrelenting siege of silent sounds. He'd tried to banish them by speaking them aloud when he was alone, but they wouldn't leave.

Making the sounds was easy; what was not easy was getting them out of his head. Other teachers had taught him how to find nourishment, how to swim, to climb, to jump from limb to limb, how to make one's self invisible, how to communicate over vast distances. The human teacher's world was small but crammed with things and the sounds to identify them. "What is this?" his teacher would say, and he would respond: "chair, table, glass, tire, track, tree, rock, water, hammer, nail – and the powerful one, e-lec-tri-ci-ty," the invisible snake that bit him when he poked a "nail" into a "socket."

**

Although brief, Fawn's encounter with the condor continued to alter the way she perceived the environment – could it have been P3? She did not know. She didn't recall seeing a wing-tag or even remember the vulture leaving its perch on the chair. But since that morning the additional period of silence seemed a gift. Awestruck by the beauty, complexity and harmony of her surroundings, she galloped through the hills like a young colt, tended the garden with vigor and cooked alongside her grandmother with a new appreciation of flavors and aroma. She watched Isabelle prepare supplies for baskets and took part when she felt confident enough to do so. Isabelle structured a frame for her to practice basic weaving. When she showed signs of frustration, her grandmother took the piece from her hands and sent her outside. What she saw there was patience: the plants grew, the spiders wove and spun, the cat watched the gopher hole.

In time, she would return to take up basketry again. If she made a miscalculation she threaded back then nudged forward at a different angle until the twists and turns of reed and stem smoothed.

She absorbed knowledge and skill; there were no written exams, just calm persistence, and freedom from speech.

Fawn bloomed in an atmosphere free of worry or fear, free from the angst to fit in.

CHAPTER 14

Fall's shorter days meant cooler nights. Dan had hoped to discover Robert sleeping in one of the cabins, or the kitchen, or the newly organized barn, but no. The boy disappeared at the end of the day's work to return an hour or so after sunrise.

Dan was putting a lot of stock in a change of season. According to the old timers, this year's heavy acorn crop was a sure sign of a harsh winter. Warmth was an enticement for any mammal, man or beast. In time, Robert would opt to come in from the cold, and long evenings in front of a warm stove would surely accelerate their ability to communicate. The boy would finally become accustomed to modern human habitat, admittedly on a very small scale. A bed, a chair, a bathroom and kitchen were part of the daily routine, whether people lived in a forest cottage or city condo. The boy still foraged for his food, apparently unwilling to risk a repeat of the consequences of eating Dan's cooking. Still, preparing a meal, sitting at the table and eating together was something Dan hoped they soon would share.

From Dan's perspective, negative incidents had been few, especially if he and Robert stayed outdoors. But one job Dan thought would go without a hitch had a surprising effect on the boy. When the time came to cut and stack wood for winter, Dan brought out the chain saw. Robert held it, assessed its weight and gingerly fingered the chain. After watching Dan mix the oil and gas, he took a whiff of the liquid and backed up, surprised, but not upset. But when Dan started the saw, Robert began to shake and, even though Dan cut the engine as soon as he noticed the boy's distress, the shaking took several minutes to subside. How could he reassure the boy that, when handled properly, the saw was not a threat, when the slightest gesture to start it up again made the boy blanch?

In the end, he gave Robert the assignment of oiling a three-story observation tower far from the location where he would be sawing. When the cutting was done, they stacked three cords in the lean-to at the back of Dan's cottage.

**

With each passing day, mimicking became easier. When the teacher pointed to an object and he made the correct sound: "truck, tire, track, road, barn, door, hammer, staple, chainsaw, oil, brush," the teacher would bare his teeth. (Unlike creatures, the boy realized baring teeth was a human signal of approval.)

Some words identified movement: run, jump, climb, stack. But words like 'work' and 'play' confused him; were they movement words? What was the difference? Learning human sound was not difficult, but why did humans do what they did? All his needs were met without these 'jobs.'

His forest home fulfilled all his needs: the safety of the heron nest, the cool water in the stream, the nourishment of crawdads and trout, lion's mane fungus and pussy-willow root, berries and watercress. Survival was not difficult, but without his creature companions, contentment remained elusive.

**

The last big project would be to repair any holes in the roofs before the rains came. Falling acorns on the cabins' metal roofing, especially when backed by strong wind, could poke holes that had to be patched with sticky goo. Once Robert learned to avoid getting the stuff on his skin, he seemed to enjoy crawling on the roofs, sealing the obvious holes on the first go-around and then checking inside for any telltale speck of light signaling a potential leak. He was fastidious with the assignment, often using a bit more "goo" than need be, but it seemed to Dan it was the most fun the boy had had since that very first day, nearly two months ago, when he sat in the old lounge chair and shifted the footrest lever time and again.

The lodge and kitchen had a roof of cedar shingle. Cupped or cracked from too much sun, a few shingles occasionally needed replacing. But the biggest problem with that roof had nothing to do with the weather. The first year Dan took over maintenance of the camp he found a sizable hole above the kitchen; a raccoon had made her way into the attic and settled in with her kits. A strong homing instinct was passed from generation to generation and every year at least one mama raccoon ripped off a substantial portion of shingles in her quest to return home to give birth.

Late one afternoon, Dan sent Robert up to remove the damaged materials from the kitchen roof. Robert hadn't known about the cause of the hole, but he knew from the scent that raccoons had claimed the attic as their den and understood the repairs he and Dan would make in the next few days would seal the entrance to the raccoon's winter home. Knowing they would emerge after dark, he returned to the lodge that evening to attempt communication with the mother. When he spotted her lumbering shape on the roof, he sat up slowly and stared in her direction. His intention was to visualize the roof repair and an alternative nesting space in an old, rarely used shed. But as soon as she saw him, the mama gave warning to her babies, and the three scurried to the ridge of the roof to avoid the human threat. The only solution was to seal the opening when the raccoons were out foraging. At least he could make sure they wouldn't be trapped.

The next afternoon, Dan came out of his cottage just as Robert was hauling the last of the roofing materials up to the repair site. "Getting ready for tomorrow?" he called.

The boy nodded, showed his teeth.

After Robert took off, Dan got to thinking about the project; maybe it was time to try something different. Before preparing dinner, he took a walk to check the random collection of building materials stored behind the barn. Yep, there it was, a good-sized sheet of corrugated metal lying beneath a pile of two-by-fours. He'd have Robert use it, rather than shingles, to repair the hole. It wouldn't be visible from the ground and could be a permanent solution.

He was pulling the metal from the bottom of the pile

when he noticed two wild animal traps stacked on top of an old freezer. Why hadn't he thought of that before? Trap, relocate. It's obvious. He hauled the piece of metal over to the lodge, then took the traps into the barn to make sure they were in working order. Just before dark, Dan baited the traps with pieces of fish and set them near the lodge. On the way back to the cottage, he had a thought that put a smile on his face. With some luck, this scheme could lead to Robert's first ride in the old pickup!

**

For the second time, the boy returned to the lodge after dark. He knew the raccoon family would be out foraging. His plan was to block the hole by stacking the repair supplies on top of it so the mother and kits would find another place to nest when they returned. He had used a ladder when he carried a bundle of shingles and the roll of tar paper up to the roof earlier that day, but now he would climb the same tree the raccoons used to access the roof. As he neared the base of the tree, he heard hissing and frantic rattling, and soon discovered the mother and one kit cowering in the corner of a wire enclosure; a second kit was trapped nearby. Where did these enclosures come from? He bent down and stared intently into the eyes of the mother. She bared her teeth, would have bitten him if she could. He ran to Dan's cottage and pounded on the door.

"What the heck?" Dan grumbled. He opened the door to see Robert, eyes wide, standing on the porch. "What?"

Robert opened the screen. He grabbed Dan's arm, anxious for assistance to free the terrified animals.

"Hold on, hold on," Dan said. "Let me get my shoes."

When they reached the base of the tree, Dan grinned. "Hey, we got 'em."

"Open," said the boy.

"No," said Dan.

Had he used the wrong word? Why didn't his teacher respond? "O-Pen!" the boy repeated.

"No."

Dan picked up the cage that held the mother and one kit, then lifted his chin toward the other cage, instructing Robert to "get that one and follow me."

The boy hesitated.

"Come on," Dan ordered.

Robert picked up the cage and followed his teacher to the barn. They each slid a door to the side and put the cages into the back of the truck. Dan reattached the battery cables and told Robert to get in the cab.

**

The boy fumbled with the door handle until the latch released and entered the moving den called 'truck.' As he pulled the door closed, he was acutely aware that he was reenacting the actions of the humans who took Buck's body away. The deep growl of the moving den so unsettled him, it was all he could do to remain passive. Even from the cab, he could sense the terror of the caged raccoons.

His teacher talked and talked and talked. He understood not a word.

At first they moved slowly on the wide rutted path, but when they turned onto the hard black surface they were swept into a current as fast as any roiling stream. Forest shapes shot past in a blur, bile rose in the boy's throat as the hurtling truck narrowly missed a startled possum and then a low flying owl in pursuit of a scrambling mouse.

When they finally slowed and stopped, his teacher leapt from the truck and set the captives free. He yearned to follow the little family scurrying into the forest. But he had been shunned; creatures no longer looked deep into his eyes to sense his intent, nor did they trust him to enter their own visions.

He was human.

**

Dan pulled the truck into the barn, disconnected the battery, slammed the hood and headed back to his cottage. He was dog-tired, wanted nothing more than to get some sleep, but the diatribe in his head would not stop. The boy must have known he had no intention of injuring those raccoons. He'd been so sure Robert would come around, be wowed by the experience of riding in a vehicle for the first time. But after they rolled out of the barn, the kid just sulked and leaned against the door.

Rocking down the rutted gravel road in first gear, Dan had launched into the story about the origin of the truck: how it had lived at the camp since 1955, how it sounded different from modern vehicles, that its low throaty rumble was like the low throaty rumble of a Harley motorcycle, how "Old Blue" had personality. Okay, maybe the kid couldn't understand a lot of what he said, but still . . .

When they reached the paved road he'd sped up, shifted through the gears, gained speed to blow out the pipes. Pretty awesome, he thought, for someone who had never had the experience. But with every bump or shift, Robert twitched and grimaced. Any other boy would have been asking questions: How hard was it to drive this cool old truck? Could he try?

Okay, he had to admit he sort of blew it on the way back, had peeled out from the side of the road, sprayed a little gravel and then hauled ass until he was forced to slow down on the road leading into camp. That's when Robert really lost it, bolted out of the cab and took off across the meadow. The kid's first ride in a vehicle had been a real bust, just like the only meal he had prepared for this surprise guest – some surprise. Dan's enthusiasm was waning. Sonja would have to come up with one heck of a pep talk to keep him interested in sticking with the, so called, Plan.

**

Even though it appeared the raccoons had not been injured, the return to camp felt as unsettling as the ride to where they'd been released. As soon as the truck slowed, the boy opened the door, jumped out, then raced down the length of the meadow before cutting up into the forest. Sprinting over fallen logs and gnarly tree roots, he ran blindly until a wisp of thorny blackberry cane snared his calf and took him to the ground. He laid there for a long time, his spirit broken under the weight of disillusionment, frustration, and the pain of torn flesh.

A whisper . . . *Telele.* The boy cocked his ear, held his breath; there it was again, a faint call . . . *Telele.* Unwrapping the vine from his bleeding leg, he stood to search for the source of the sound. He was surprised to realize he had been here before. Condor had led him here; he had climbed onto

Buck's back next to that very tree. The black oak, now bare of leaves, emitted a vibrant glowing energy. As he approached the pulsating trunk, his heart took up its rhythm; the roots drew his energy down, grounding him firmly to Mother Earth. In that blessed quietude, he felt Feline's presence. *Your destiny and ours are entwined; we have not abandoned you. Telele* . . . Human voices . . . *Telele.* In the misty distance he saw a village: men, women, children clustered near bark dens, an ancient human family whose essence inhabited the fiber of this land, interwoven with the intricate web of source. He walked toward them, but with each step they drifted, like smoke, just beyond his reach.

"My name, Telele," he said, and with that awareness he made a vow to stand as fast as the Great Black Oak.

CHAPTER 15

The curriculum at Alex's prep school was demanding. He liked that. It kept his mind off of the quiet chaos of home. Home, what a joke. If he just had a sibling; even a dog would help. But pets made his mother nervous. Lots of things made his mother nervous. He did not, however, make his mother nervous. He came home when he said he would, got good grades, treated the help kindly. His friends were happy to have him over to their houses and didn't expect a return invitation.

Then there was Father, Congressman Phillip Perry. Father and Mother and Alex lived together in a house where luxurious cars pulled inside the gates, cars driven by chauffeurs delivering important people, people with influence and lots and lots of money. Should Alex arrive home when a guest was present, he was required to make not just an appearance, but a good impression.

It would go like this: "Hey, son, I'd like you to meet my good friend so and so." Like his father, so and so would sport an ingratiating grin and a solid handshake. Alex would say,

"It's a pleasure to meet you. Please excuse me; I'm on my way to a basketball game." Neither Father nor his guest would mention it wasn't basketball season. He could say anything, really: "I'm going to see a lion tamer. I'm headed out to sea."

This Saturday morning, the big, elegant house was completely quiet. Alex slumped at his desk and, avoiding the history textbook in front of him, gazed around his room. Clothes were piling up; bowls, spoons, cups and glasses littered all flat surfaces. In his quest to squelch one of the things that irritated him most, he'd managed to convince his mother to exclude his room from the constant straightening and scrubbing the staff carried out in the rest of the house. How was he supposed to have any privacy, he'd argued, with maids going through his drawers, vacuuming under the bed, turning his mattress? He knew if she caught a glimpse of this mess she'd send the staff back in.

Prying himself out of the chair, he resolved to put things in order. After an hour of organizing, returning dirty dishes to the kitchen, and scrubbing the bathroom, he took advantage of the momentum, finished his homework and checked his e-mail; still no word from Ranger Dan. It had been nearly three months since Alex left Muir Camp. He decided to initiate contact, and composed an e-mail saying that, after writing a report on the California condor, he realized it was impossible to have seen one in the Central Sierra Nevada mountains. On the other hand, after studying photos of bears, he was convinced the eyes staring at him from that oak tree belonged to a cub, a cub that was probably eating like crazy right now, getting ready to hibernate.

Ah, Muir Camp. No house in Pacific Heights could come close to the comfort in those cabins. Hikes, cooking over a fire, playing cards, talking late into the night with his cabin mates; he was never lonely there. Logging off, Alex looked around his tidy room, then grabbed his backpack. He had to get out of here. The ocean would lift his spirits.

Alex liked coves, he liked tide pools, but this pent-up feeling called for a wide open, long stretch of sand, a run 'til you drop kind of beach, Ocean Beach at the west end of Golden Gate Park. In the kitchen he grabbed a few snacks and two water bottles. He'd be gone a while and nobody would notice.

It took a few bus connections to get to Ocean Beach. By the time he jumped off at the last stop, Alex had obsessed about his home life to the point of, if he was honest, drowning in self-pity: *My parents don't care, they never listen, if I only had a brother, heck even a sister would be okay, they should just send me to a boarding school.* He was on his way to a long afternoon of brooding.

And then he saw her.

Actually, he saw a swath of amazing color a few hundred feet down the wide walkway that separated the road from the strand. Were those chairs? Metal ones as it turned out, six of them, awash in reds, yellows, purples, greens and swaths of fluorescent orange. They were festooned with flowers, rainbows, peace signs and butterflies, a vision of a party in Rio, Kingston, or Ensenada. As he got closer, Alex could hear the sound of reggae. He could not stop smiling. For the first time since he'd left the house he was fully aware of the misty quality of the light, the salty smell of the ocean, the rhythmic sound of crashing waves, the high pitched squawking of seagulls. But when he got close to the chairs, he saw something that actually took his breath away. A tall slender goddess was sliding off the four-foot wall on the sea-side of the walkway. He took in every detail of the long, muscular dark brown leg stretched toward the sidewalk. His whole body lit up.

Her chairs were for sale. If one was available, you were welcome to sit. If you settled down with a look that said 'this fits,' or she suspected you might be about to ask 'how much,' she would offer a cola or lemonade from an ice-chest next to the boom box.

After watching money change hands five times and chair after chair disappear, Alex handed the goddess twenty dollars. "Could you hold this for me? I'll pay the rest when I pick it up . . . I mean, I can't take it right now. Uh . . . I jogged over here, so I don't have my car."

She smiled, took his money and handed him a bright pink card with e-mail address and cell phone number. "I hold two weeks only."

Oh, that accent – Jamaican.

"Don't you want my name?" Alex asked.

She shook her large hoop earrings. "I don't need no name."

Alex blushed. His face felt hot. "Okay then," he said, "Gotta go."

He jogged to the nearest opening in the wall, took a long run on the packed sand near the water, then headed back to the bus stop with a grin on his face and a song playing in his head. *Don't worry, 'bout a thing, every little thing's gonna be alright.*

"Good afternoon, Master Alex. Would you please be so kind as to brush the sand off your feet before you mess up my clean floor?"

Alex should be mad; he'd asked her to stop calling him that at least three years ago. But mad wasn't possible because it was Lucia, and she loved him, and her accent was music to his ears. Old women with accents, young women with accents, he tried to suppress a smile.

"Lucia, please."

"I like the way it sounds."

"I don't."

"Haven't you seen Downtown Abbey?"

"Yes, Mother loves it. But this isn't one hundred years ago England, and I don't wish it was."

"Have you noticed the dresses?"

"If you stop calling me Master Alex, I'll get you one, I promise."

"You are growing up to be charming, like your father," she teased.

"You think my father is charming?"

"Well, not to me, but . . ."

"Me either," said Alex. He started up the stairs to his room. "I'm going to take a shower. What time is dinner?"

"Your father wants to eat at six-thirty. He has a meeting at eight."

"Do we have company?"

"No."

"Good. Is Mother going to eat with us?"

"Yes."

At six twenty-five Alex's mom opened his door. "Dear, would you walk me to the dining room?"

"Sure," said Alex, "I'll just turn off the stereo."

Mother followed him into the room in a perfume cloud. "I can't believe you wanted that old turntable."

"Vinyl is popular again. I'm glad Dad saved these records."

"That was Bob Marley, wasn't it?" she said, walking back toward the door. "He died because he didn't take care of cancer in his toe or something." She waited in the hallway while Alex slipped the album in its cover and left the room. "It's a good reminder," she continued, "never let a persistent pain go on too long without doing something about it."

The three of them sat at one end of the dining table where several platters of food awaited. They served themselves when they didn't have company.

"So," Father said, "I hear you dug out my old turntable and some records. Find anything you like?"

Mother answered for Alex. "Bob Marley."

"Really," said Father. "I always wished I'd seen him in person."

Thinking he detected wistfulness in his father's statement, Alex perked up. "I saw a Jamaican woman selling hand-painted chairs at the beach today." Only the sound of knives and forks against china followed what turned out to be a dead end subject.

Father broke the silence with a standard question. "How's school?"

"I did a report on the California Condor," Alex answered. "I thought I saw one last summer at camp, but now

I know that couldn't have happened. They live near the coast in California, near the Grand Canyon, too."

His mother thoroughly chewed a bite of roast beef before her comment. "They are so ugly."

"They're huge," Alex said. "They can have up to a nine and a half foot wing span, and they like to play!"

His mother shook her head. "That's just anthropomorphizing."

Father gave Alex a little wink. "Big word, dear," he said.

Mother smiled. "Thank you."

"I don't see why so much money is spent to hatch the damn things." Perry's brow furrowed with disapproval. "Why not just stuff the few that are left and put them in museums next to the dinosaurs."

Alex excused himself, returned to his room and turned on his computer.

Dear Alex,

I'm so glad you got in touch. I wish I had a better excuse for not getting back to you, but I've been busy and just plain forgot. I'd like to hear more about the report you made on the California Condor. Can you send it to me as an attachment? As for the bear, you may have been right. There have been some sightings near here recently.

I've been thinking about having a four day co-ed retreat for a small group of campers from last summer. We would work together to brainstorm a program for those of you who are interested in pursuing careers in forestry, ecology, geology and other related professions. Maybe during Christmas vacation? All expenses will be covered. I'm hoping to provide transportation from the bay area, too. Just eight participants, so we can get everybody into a van.

Interested?

Dan

**

Dan surprised himself when he mentioned the retreat in his e-mail to Alex. Apparently he was ready to take action. The idea had begun to percolate after relocating the raccoon family. Robert had been sullen ever since. He showed up every day, but Dan sensed a pulling away. The boy had never formulated many sentences. Now there was even a marked lack of interest in learning new words.

He ran it by Sonja. "I think he needs to see people his own age."

"But he's not ready; how is that going to work?"

"I don't intend for him to meet them," Dan said. "I want him to observe them. He's a master at staying out of sight. Maybe it will spur him on to try again. I really think it could make a difference."

"How many kids are you talking about?" Sonja asked.

"I'm thinking eight total, four girls, four boys."

"So he'll see the female of the species at last."

"Might spark his interest," Dan said. "I was wondering if you and your daughter would like to be part of it. I'm trying to do this on a shoestring budget, and I'd need to have a female counselor. It could be a little vacation for you."

"Fawn is with her grandmother right now. I'll get back to you on that."

Sonja sent a letter to her mother-in-law explaining Dan's proposal. Word came back that Isabelle thought it was a sound idea. Fawn was doing well. "In fact," she wrote, "I think it's a perfect segue for her to return to life with her peers."

With just six weeks until the proposed dates, Dan got busy and recruited three other girls and four boys, including Alex. The date was set for the last four days of December.

Dan had a few fireworks stashed away, illegal because of fire danger on the Fourth of July, but a fun way to celebrate the New Year.

CHAPTER 16

It rained and rained, and rained some more. Sonja had reserved a van to transport the eight kids to Muir camp for the winter retreat. Interacting with big vultures, no problem, but the thought of keeping eight young people busy for four days, not to mention a half day in the car each direction, made her anxious. And the weather had her on edge.

She called Dan on Christmas day with detectable panic in her voice. "What's the weather like up there?"

"Snowing!" he said, enthusiastically.

"What are we going to do?"

"Have a good time. I've contacted everybody, told them to bring boots and long underwear; they'll be fine."

"Will I need chains?"

"Maybe," Dan said.

"I don't know about this."

"Ah, come on. It's a learning opportunity."

"But–"

"Tell you what. I'll contact Alex Perry and have him study a you-tube video about putting on chains. If you need them, enlist the kids to help and put Alex in charge."

Sonja let out an exasperated breath. "If you say so."

"If it's too stormy when you get to town, just call and I'll drive down to help."

"How long does it take for you to get to town?"

"Depends."

"And where does one haggard counselor and eight kids wait in a town that size?"

"We'll cross that bridge if we come to it. Stop worrying; this is going to be a great weekend. For the first time in a long time, Robert is looking forward to something." As Dan knew it would, the mention of Robert did the trick.

"Okay," she said, "I'll see you day after tomorrow."

A back up beeper sounded its warning as Sonja squeezed the over-sized vehicle into the loading zone in front of the San Francisco Ferry building. Fawn checked out the group waiting to load their backpacks and sleeping bags into the rented van. "Mom, can I stay up front?"

Sonja pushed the gear shift lever into park and turned off the engine. "I think it would be better if you sat in the back. It will give you a chance to get acquainted."

Fawn groaned. She hadn't had contact with someone her own age for nearly four months and, truth be told, she'd never been all that great at socializing. "Okay," she agreed, "but could we avoid mentioning you're my mom."

"Good idea. One thing's for sure, no one would guess. I'll have to remember to tell Dan not to mention it."

As soon as the van was parked, Fawn jumped out to open the side and back doors. Three girls and four boys grabbed their gear, eager to get out of the rain.

"Climb on in," Sonja called, "and let's mix it up back there; alternate girls and boys in the seats, okay?"

"Why?" The boy who asked the question wore thick glasses, had a full set of braces and was the shortest of the group.

"And you would be?" Sonja asked.

"Fee . . . well Felix, but I go by Fee."

"Here's the deal, Fee. Since this is a co-ed retreat and we will be forming co-ed teams for the different activities, it seems to me it would be a good idea to start right now. Make sense?"

"I guess," he said.

"Now, why don't you come on up here and sit in front with me." Felix jumped into the front seat with a wiry grin.

Fawn helped stow the gear in the back, then stood on the sidewalk while the others climbed in. Every girl, it seemed, was waiting to see where Alex would sit, but he made a point of hanging back until everyone but Fawn had taken a seat. He motioned for her to go ahead of him, squeezed in next to her and pulled the door closed. Tall for his age with curly blonde hair and piercing blue eyes, it was all Fawn could do not to stare. She was in heaven.

Before pulling into traffic on the Embarcadero, Sonja turned around in her seat and addressed the group. "Hi everyone, I'm Sonja Henderson. I'm an ornithologist. I teach at Cal Poly in San Luis Obispo and, two days a week, monitor California Condors in Los Padres National Forest. Dan Fisk and I worked together years ago. When he decided to organize this retreat he asked if I would team up with him. I understand one of you thought you saw a condor at camp last summer."

"That was me," said the young man sitting next to Fawn.

"And you are?"

"I'm Alex Perry. I've done some research since then. I realize I couldn't have seen a condor in the Sierras."

"Still," Sonja said, "it caused you to investigate, and that's exactly what we want to encourage all of you to do in the next few days. Investigation makes for more accurate information. Being proved wrong is just as, or maybe more important than, proving yourself right. Thank you, Alex. Now, before we get started I'd like each of you to introduce yourself to the group and say one thing that's on your mind. Felix, how about you go first."

Felix turned shyly toward the back of the van. "I'm Felix. I live in Concord. I hope I have enough warm clothes."

"That's on my mind too," Sonja said. "Alright, let's hear from the back seat."

"Hi, I'm Stacy. I'm from San Francisco. I hope there's snow at camp because I've never seen any."

"Well," Sonja said, "I talked to Dan yesterday and it was snowing, but I don't know how much or whether it stuck. Next."

"I'm Jeremy. I live in San Francisco in the Richmond district. I'm concerned about how warm my Dad's old down sleeping bag is. Man, I hate to be cold."

Sonja was glad she could alleviate Jeremy's concern. "You'll be happy to know there are plenty of blankets at the camp. Next."

The tallest of the girls, with corn-rowed hair sporting

several colors of neon-bright highlights said, "Hi, I'm Alisha. I missed camp last year, but I've stayed in touch with Ranger Dan, and I'm really excited he asked if I would like to come on this retreat."

Sonja looked to the other boy in the back seat, round as a butterball with big dimples and a sweet smile. "Hi," he said, "I'm Nate." He glanced at Stacy. "I've never seen snow either."

The kids in the middle seat followed suit. "I'm June. I've been to camp two summers. I think this is a great way to end the year."

Fawn was next. "Hi, I'm Fawn. I'm looking forward to the activities."

"Alex," Sonja said, "Is there anything else you want to share?"

"I've been to Muir Camp three years in a row, but never in winter, and I think it's a great way to end the year, too."

"Okay then," Sonja concluded, "we're on our way." She turned on the blinker and eased into the post-Christmas traffic.

The group in the back chatted amiably as Sonja snaked her way out of the city and negotiated thick traffic on the five-lane freeway across the San Joaquin Valley. When they began to climb into the foothills there was plenty of snow, but even on the last leg of the journey, the thirty miles of curvy narrow road to Muir Camp was easily passable without the dreaded chains.

If Alex hadn't recognized several clues, (an old bridge, a lightning struck tree on the right, a snag resembling the head of a buck on the left) Sonja would likely have missed the turn. "Slow down," he called from the back. "There!" The gravel road was pocked with rain filled holes. Sonja steered the bulky vehicle skillfully between and around them. When they passed by the Native Peoples Village, the only indication of its existence was a group of white mounds of various shapes and sizes surrounded by thickly frosted trees. But when the cabins came into view, the kids had no trouble identifying their favorites, several commenting on the advantages of certain locations: close to the bathrooms (the girls,) far from Dan's cottage, (the boys.)

"You haven't been here before, have you?" June asked Fawn.

"I have," Fawn answered, "just not during camping season." Fortunately, that was answer enough. Just as well, Fawn thought. I'd have a hard time explaining that I, or a different of version of I, hadn't slept in a cabin at Muir Camp but on the dirt floor of one of the bark dwellings . . . next to wild boy.

**

It took much more than the first winter storm to coax Robert to spend time inside Dan's cottage. The boy had an amazing tolerance for cold. After a lifetime of traversing the landscape barefoot, his thickly callused soles were as impenetrable as the soles of hiking boots. His limber frame and supple muscles were encased in thick, brown skin and, in the past few weeks, a dense layer of almost invisible, downy hair had appeared; no wonder the elements were of little concern. But when a week-long series of unrelenting storms drove daytime temperatures into the teens, and nighttime temperatures hovering near zero, Robert began to stay overnight in the cottage, sleeping on the rug next to the wood stove. When the weather returned to milder temperatures, Dan sensed it was the need for companionship that caused Robert to settle into the cabin night after night.

Closer contact had accelerated the boy's language skills immensely. Scattered nouns and verbs became simple, if not grammatically correct, sentences; sentences followed one another into better developed thoughts. Sonja's advice to leave the radio on had helped as well.

"He'll learn quickly if he's immersed in word sounds, even if he doesn't understand," she'd told Dan. "It's like singing in a way, the rhythm, the intonation, it just soaks in."

But there would come a time each evening when Robert would start to show signs of agitation, grinding his teeth or unconsciously tapping his fingers on the floor. Suddenly, he would jump up and turn the radio off, a relief to them both.

The food issue hadn't changed. The boy continued to find his nourishment elsewhere but would, occasionally, bring it to the cottage and eat with Dan. The other end of that process, so to speak, was the only major source of conflict since the raccoon incident. Robert had entered the cabin carrying a trout wrapped in what he now referred to as his 'blue skin.' Apparently the fish had slipped out of the blanket, hit the ground and was covered with dirt and leaves. Fish in hand, he headed for the bathroom. When Dan heard splashing he went in to see the fish being rinsed in the toilet. Dan explained what a toilet was used for. Robert was incredulous and asked for the explanation again. When Dan explained a second time Robert scowled in fierce disapproval. Defecation in water was completely intolerable to the boy, and no amount of education, including a detailed drawing of soil pipe, septic tank and leach lines, softened the judgment. Robert was disgusted, horrified, and Dan made sure he was alone in the cottage if he needed to make use of the facility.

A warm shower was another matter. Robert took them often. When Dan showed him a catalog with photos of scrubbed clean boys his own age, he could tell the boy was interested. Soap or shampoo, however, was out of the question. Artificial smells sent him into a paroxysm of coughs and sneezes.

Until just recently, the only piece of clothing Robert had worn was the shorts he'd plucked from the clothesline. Now, he had a small chest of drawers with underwear, long pants, shirts and sweaters, all pillaged from the lost and found box. A jacket his size hung on a peg near the door. Shoes and socks? Well, that just wasn't going to happen. He'd tried some on, limped around the room for a minute, then chucked them under Dan's bed.

As Christmas approached, Dan pondered whether he should try to explain the idea of holiday, the customs humans enacted year after year, but decided against it. Instead, since Robert had shown an interest in music whenever it came from the radio, Dan pulled out his guitar and a small wooden flute from the back of his closet. The flute proved to be the perfect instrument for Robert. With his keen sense of hearing and nimble fingers he caught on quickly; before long the two managed to play a simple holiday tune together and, to Dan's delight, instead of an uncomfortable grimace, the boy had actually smiled.

Late in the day on the twenty-first of December, Robert

urged Dan to follow him to the sky tower. When they reached the top, the boy faced the star around which the whole planetary system revolved. He rotated ninety degrees to the right, once, twice, three times, returning to his original position just as the glowing sphere dipped below the horizon. As fanning rays of light bathed the clouds in a stunning array of color, he thrust his arms up and down like wings, then dropped into a deep squat, drew his arms close to his body and ducked his head to make himself as compact as possible. Dan stood silent, mesmerized. He would never forget winter solstice, 2012.

One week later, the two were sitting at the kitchen table when Robert cocked his ear and pronounced, "They are here." Dan rose to answer the knock at the cottage door, and the boy made a quick exit out the bathroom window.

CHAPTER 17

Sonja and the eight campers entered Dan's cottage with wet boots and dripping jackets. They removed their shoes, lined them up near the wood stove and hung their jackets on pegs by the door. Without thinking, Fawn ran into the bathroom, found a ragged towel under the sink and wiped the places where the floor was wet. Realizing she had made herself at home without asking, she sat down at the table with the dirty towel on her lap.

"Here," Dan said to Fawn, "Let me take that." He reached for the muddy towel, then turned to the group. "Fawn has just given an example of taking initiative. I'm not saying I don't want you to ask before doing something, but if you see what needs to be done, and you know it doesn't really require asking, just do it. In the next four days we want to encourage awareness, investigation, action and cooperation."

"On that note," Fawn said, shyly, "I wanted to mention that the bathroom window is wide open. It's really freezing in there. Should I have closed it?"

Dan hoped Robert would return to sleep inside; the

window was the most discreet way for him to enter the cottage. "Thanks for asking," he said. "It shouldn't be wide open, but I like to keep it cracked a little. I'll take care of that right now."

When Dan returned to the living room, Nate verbalized what was on everyone's mind. "It sure smells good in here." "I'm glad to hear it," Dan said. "Let's eat."

Wild turkey soup simmered on the stove; a loaf of Dan's home-baked sourdough sat on the table. They all settled down in the warm quarters to enjoy the meal. After dinner, Dan passed out pencils and paper, asking everyone to answer two questions: What has been your favorite experience at Muir camp? In what ways do you relate to nature when you are not at camp?

"Does anyone want to share what they wrote?" Dan asked.

Felix's earlier hesitancy to socialize disappeared. He spoke of his encounter last summer with a possum. "It was well after dark, and a few of us decided to hike up to the sky tower."

Dan shook his head. "It's a wonder you didn't get into poison oak."

Reminded of the rule about hiking without a counselor after dark, Felix blushed. "We could see well enough to stay on the trail," he said, sheepishly. "The moon was almost full."

Dan smiled; Felix continued. "Anyway, on the way back the other guys ran ahead, trying to ditch me I guess, so I slowed way down. If I hadn't, I would have missed this beady-eyed, ratty looking animal almost the size of a cat. He walked right in front of me; neither one of us was moving very fast."

He told the others that was when he became interested in the much maligned family of rodents. "There are lots of rats and mice in the alley behind my house. They use the overhead wires like freeways."

Alisha told about a class assignment at her school where the kids were asked to observe wildlife. "What wildlife?" she'd protested. "We live in the city." The teacher suggested they find an anthill. "I was just blown away when I took the time to watch how ants work together, how complex their culture is." She had learned that ants maintain 'dairy farms' of aphids. "Wildlife is everywhere," she said, "even when we cover it up with concrete and asphalt."

By ten, everyone was ready to get some sleep. Dan had put a small electric heater in each of the cabins. "It won't be toasty," he said, "but you won't freeze. Cabin four for you boys, eight for the girls. You know the way. There are extra blankets and pillows at the end of the bunks. See you in the lodge at 7:30."

"Where will I be staying?" Sonja asked.

"There's a great little guest room next to the kitchen. I've warmed that up too."

Robert did not return that night. Dan laid awake for a long time, wishing the boy was sleeping on the rug near the stove and questioning, just a little, his decision to set up the retreat.

**

The sweet scent of moist cedar bark permeated the interior of the snow-covered sweat lodge. Buck guarded the low opening; his presence not only blocked the wind, but served as reminder of the boy's covenant with The Council. When First Peoples called to him on the night of the caged raccoons, their village was enveloped in a smoky cloud. The boy had moved carefully toward it, but the village and its inhabitants stayed just beyond his reach. When it all vanished, he realized he'd been coaxed, step by step, to where Buck's hide, head down, horns nearly touching the ground, hung between two magenta limbs of manzanita. He had carefully removed it from the scaffold of branches, carried it back to camp and stored it in the rafters of the round house. This morning he'd retrieved the skin to cover the opening of the sweat lodge.

It upset him to realize he had already become less tolerant of the cold. Dressed in long pants, shirt and jacket, only his calloused feet were free. Curling into the indention made by the sweat lodge fire, he thought about Dan's instructions. For the next few days he was to stay out of sight and observe the ways of the young humans he must learn to emulate.

After the visitors first arrived he'd settled into the crotch of a tree with a view through the window over Dan's desk. He'd recognized the tallest boy as the one who had stalked him near the stream months before. There were other boys, two with dark hair, one with hair the color of a sunset. And there were females: one with skin darker than his own and as tall as the tallest boy, a short one with straight black hair, one with a cap, and one with shiny metal in her ears. He was intrigued, but when they stopped moving around the cottage he had retreated to the sweat lodge.

**

Dan awoke before dawn. Lying in bed, he remembered Sonja's request. "Please don't mention Fawn is my daughter," she'd asked. "It will be easier for both of us." It wouldn't be much of a challenge; they looked nothing alike. At six a.m. he dressed and headed for the lodge, intending to build a roaring fire and was surprised to see Sonja already feeding more wood onto a well-established bed of coals.

"I started it last night," she said. "Hope you don't mind."

"Not at all," Dan replied. "I'll assign fire tenders for the rest of the retreat. I'd like to keep this space warm. After we eat I thought we would send the kids out to find walking sticks, then set up a space in here where they can customize them."

"Sounds fun."

"They'll be great for snow hiking."

Sonja sat on the hearth. "And Robert?" she asked.

"He's likely watching us now," Dan said. "I won't be privy to what he's seen until everyone is gone."

The heavy lodge door opened, and they both turned to see Alex walk in. "I was thinking I'd be the one to get the fire going," he said.

Dan smiled. "Sonja beat us both to the punch."

The walking stick activity took up most of the morning. Every camper took the time to find the right hefty stick, carefully minding the length and the handhold. Then they returned to the lodge to carve and decorate with a variety of found objects, adhering them with string or pine pitch. Following a slide presentation on prints, the group enthusiastically headed back out into the snow where they saw clear evidence of wild turkey, fox, deer, rabbit, and what appeared to be a large species of cat.

At the recreated Native Peoples village, Fee suggested they poke their sticks into the snow to see how many bowl shaped indentions they could find in the grinding rock there. Fawn lagged behind in hopes of spotting Robert. She was sure she detected his scent, but hesitated to follow her nose for fear someone would follow her.

**

Robert sat frustrated in the center of the sweat lodge. Prints were starkly revealing in the unmarked snow and his barefoot ones would attract unwanted attention; he was stuck. His body ached from lack of movement. He should have brought the dreaded shoes he'd thrown under Dan's bed. He knew the campers were clustered at the large grinding rock, but all he could do was listen.

**

"All right, folks. Let's get those lunches packed. We're going to the sky tower."

The group's reaction to the announcement was mixed. Some hadn't slept so well and wanted to stay in the warm lodge to fine tune their walking sticks. "Fine tuning walking sticks is using them," Dan said. "Make sure you have your sketch books in your day packs, and put a few of those plastic sandwich bags in, too. We might find some scat to collect." All knew better than to groan at that one.

Fawn saw Sonja disappear through a door at the far corner of the kitchen. While the other campers were busy preparing for the hike, she quietly slipped away, seeking a few minutes alone with her mother. Sonja's back was to the door when Fawn stepped into the room.

"Mom," Fawn said . . . No response. "Sonja?"

Sonja turned and smiled at her daughter. "That a girl."

Fawn looked around the sunny space. "Nice room."

"Pretty lucky, huh, how was the cabin?"

"I didn't sleep much, but it's okay. Alisha and I took the top bunks. Did you notice how tall she is? I think she might have Alex beat."

"It's close ... Your walking stick turned out great."

"Yeah."

"Okay, time's a wasting, what did you really want to talk about?"

"I think I've figured something out."

"What?"

"Why there's no trace of Robert."

"Fawn, he's not supposed to be seen, he's supposed to watch."

"He's not watching."

"How do you know that?"

"I just know.

"Fawn, did you . . . "

"Of course not, the box is still in my closet at home, and besides, I promised Grandmother."

"Then what are you saying?"

"I have a good idea where he is, and I know he feels stuck there."

"Go on."

"At first I didn't understand how that could happen, but when I was scouting around Dan's cottage for tracks, I spotted Robert's leading away from the bathroom window."

"How did you know they were his?"

"His tracks are clear as day. They're really wide with splayed toes and nail marks, sort of like a bear. He doesn't wear shoes, and I bet he's realized he can't stay out of sight without them."

"Sounds logical."

"Do you think Dan has tried to get Robert to wear shoes?" Fawn asked.

"Undoubtedly."

"Tell him to leave shoes for Robert at the entrance to the sweat lodge."

"Okay." Sonja agreed. She glanced at her watch. "You'd better get back out there."

"Are you going on the hike with us?"

"Yes," Sonja said, "and since Dan should take care of Robert's problem right away, I'll need to be the one to get the group started." She shook her head. "I have no idea where the sky tower is."

"Most of the kids have hiked there before. We'll find it. One thing's for sure, it'll be a cinch getting back. Tracks are like neon signs in snow."

**

A human was approaching. The boy crawled to the back of the sweat lodge where the domed roof met the ground. A gloved hand slipped a pair of boots past Buck's hide and set them down near the entrance. When he retrieved the boots Robert found a pair of socks in one and, in the other, the tool he'd seen Dan use to shorten toe and finger claws. To tolerate the boots he would have to use that tool. It wasn't easy, but he did the deed, pulled on the thick socks, forced his feet into the boots and limped into a crisp, sun-drenched day. Next, he collected an array of rocks, arranging them into random solid stepping surfaces, six to eight feet apart. They would enable him to go from the sweat lodge to a dense copse of nearby pine without touching the ground. Using a branch, he swept away any trace of prints, then he leapt from stone to stone to the nearest tree, scurried up to get a view and spotted the whole group of young humans weaving uphill toward the sky tower.

**

Alex took the lead, and Sonja took last place in case some of the hikers fell behind. Being at the rear made the going easy, but even though Fee was directly in front of Sonja on the packed path, his slow gate and thick glasses made him seemed confused, not unlike his description of the possum. It wasn't long before Dan came up behind them with a cheery, "Well, hello you two."

Sonja gave him an inquiring look; he nodded then reached into his backpack and pulled out a pair of snow shoes. "Hey, Fee. Want to give these a try?"

Fee slipped on the lightweight, modern version of the old standard and tested them off the packed trail. "Wow, these are awesome."

"I'm going to catch up with the others," Dan said. "If you guys have any trouble, give me a holler."

Sonja put two fingers at the edges of her mouth and let out a shrill whistle.

"Whoa," said Dan, "Save that for emergencies, okay?"

"Okay."

"Can you teach me how to do that?" Fee asked.

"Later," Sonja said. "We don't want to sound an alarm right now."

"Right," Fee agreed. "I'd really like to get it down though. You never know when you'll need it . . . and it's so cool."

By the time Sonja and Fee reached the sky tower, the others were standing around the perimeter at the top, ankle deep in snow, eating lunch. Fee took off the snowshoes and left them at the bottom of the steps to begin the forty-two step climb. By the last step his muscles were so shaky he plopped down in the snow and gobbled his sandwich.

"Okay, everyone, we're going to do an exercise," Dan announced. "Line up on this side of the platform alternating male and female."

Fee pried himself up and squeezed in between Fawn and June.

"The snow will be an extra challenge with this one," Dan said. "I want you to stand so your feet are touching the feet of the person next to you. The task is to walk as a group to the other side of the platform while keeping your feet connected. If any part of the bond is broken, everyone backs up and starts again."

There were smirks.

"Ready? . . . Did I hear a yes?"

A couple of the kids nodded, a couple hesitantly responded with a weak affirmative.

"Loud and clear, please," Dan said. "Now, are you ready?"

"YES!"

"That's the spirit. Okay, go!"

In seconds the group had fallen apart.

Alex stepped forward. "We need structure. I'll call out left, right, left, right, and we'll move in unison." They lined up again and fell apart as quickly as before. Alex was quick to state his displeasure. "What's wrong with you guys?"

"Excuse me!" Alisha walked up to Alex and looked him straight in the eye. "Don't you know when you say 'right' every other person has to move their left foot, and every other person just happens to be female!"

Dan jumped in. "Okay, at ease. Let's talk."

"Alex thinks he's the big man here," Alisha said.

June came to Alex's defense. "He just wanted to give his idea a try."

Alex glared at Alisha. "At least I *had* an idea."

Alisha returned to her spot next to Nate. Complaints and possible solutions rumbled down the line. Dan and Sonja were waiting to see if the group could resolve the conflict themselves when Fee piped in. "My pants are soaking wet; I'm freezing. Do you guys care if I start back?"

Dan glanced at Sonja. "I don't know."

Sonja looked at Fee. "You know to follow the tracks, right?"

"Of course," Fee said. "They're really obvious."

Sonja nodded her head. "I think it would be okay."

"Are you sure you can't wait?" Dan asked.

The blue cast of Fee's lips said it all. Dan took a large handkerchief out of his pocket and tied it around Fee's face.

"All right," Dan said. "You'll feel better when you start moving. Use the snowshoes. Going downhill, you should make it to the lodge in no more than fifteen minutes. We won't be far behind."

Fee headed down the steps, and the others continued to discuss the best course of action to complete the exercise. They all agreed successful completion, not speed, was the goal, and that a fairly uniform amount of pressure was really important. They lined up, made sure the foot against foot pressure was about the same across the line, took another shot at it, and failed again.

**

The boy had a perfect view of the campers at the sky tower. He marveled at the variety of size and shape, at the pitches and tones of their voices, and the variety of clothes they wore. He was equally interested in the shoe-covers the smallest boy had left at the bottom of the steps, so he shinnied down the tree, put them on and walked several yards on the unpacked snow on the north side the tower. After putting the shoe-coverings back where he'd found them, he noticed that the whole group had gathered on one side of the platform, and chose a different tree to continue his observations. He watched them form a line then struggle to move forward with their feet pressed together. Moments later the tallest male and the tallest female stood face to face and growled. The group lined up again, apparently determined to repeat the awkward movement. Human behavior was such a mystery. He hoped Dan could help him understand the ritual.

**

It was nearing time to leave when Fawn came up with a solution. "I think we should count, starting at one end of the line and make one move per number."

"Huh?"

"Like a wave," she said. "The person at the left end takes a step forward with a single foot, that's one. Then she and the person next to her take a step together to match the first one, that's two. Then the next set of feet, three, and all the way across; we do it over and over until we reach the other side."

It was a slow process but, to everyone's relief, it worked. Dan was pleased, Sonja proud.

"Now that you've solved the problem," Dan said, "do you want to do it one more time before we go?"

"YES!"

The 'one last time' wasn't much quicker, but was executed more smoothly, fulfilling the objective of bonding the group and boosting their confidence as a unit.

"Great job," Dan said. "Grab your gear. We'll discuss what we've learned at dinner."

CHAPTER 18

The boy tired of watching the platform and decided to make his exit before the group started back for the lodge. He knew the campers would return exactly as they had come; his bare footprints on a pristine alternate route would pose no problem. Taking great pleasure in removing the pinching shoes, he stuffed the socks inside and bounded down the hill feeling as free as the rabbits leaping through the snow ahead of him. One of the rabbits stopped and sniffed the air. The boy smelled it too; a bobcat was close by. The rabbit took off; the bobcat appeared and gave chase. When the rabbit disappeared under a fallen tree, the bobcat sat patiently next to the log, waiting for another opportunity to pounce.

The sun was close to setting, but he was in no hurry to return to the sweat lodge. Observing his human counterparts unsettled him. He understood the rabbit and the bobcat; their behavior exemplified the web of interconnection. By comparison, humans seemed stilted, disconnected. How does one survive being disconnected?

Confusion . . .

It made him feel all the more separate.

**

As soon as the sun started its descent, the temperature dropped precipitously, was downright frigid by the time the group arrived back at the lodge. Everyone shucked their jackets, shoes, gloves and hats near the well-banked stove in the main room then gathered in the kitchen, eager to get dinner underway. Dan and Sonja retreated to the dining area to discuss the afternoon's events.

"I saw that look of pride on your face when Fawn figured out the exercise," Dan said.

"Just being a mom. Pretty smart, huh."

"And thoughtful." Dan took a quick look around the room. "I guess Fee made good use of the snowshoes."

Sonja glanced at her watch. "I wonder how fast he got back . . . a twenty minute head start; he's probably had a shower already."

"I think I'll let him keep the snowshoes for the rest of the retreat," Dan said. "He's such a trooper; he deserves a boost."

Sonja stood up. "He may not know the others have started dinner. I think I'll go see how he's coming along."

"No, I'll go," Dan said. "He might be in the bathroom or something."

As soon as he stepped outside, Dan felt uneasy. At first he just ambled, but was running by the time he approached the cabin. "Fee, we're back . . . Hey, Fee . . . Fee?" Dan burst through the cabin door, threw aside the sleeping bags on all four bunks, then bolted to the boy's bathhouse to check every stall and shower. When he returned to the lodge he went straight to the kitchen. "Has anyone seen Fee since we got back?" No one responded.

Sonja saw his concern as soon as he walked into the room. "He has to be here somewhere," she said. "The trail was perfectly obvious."

"Believe me, he's not here," Dan replied. "What was I thinking, letting him start off alone like that?"

"You can't blame yourself; I'm the one who thought he'd be fine."

"Let's get Alex in here." Dan said. "He knows this camp almost as well as I do...I could use his help."

"And Fawn," Sonja suggested.

"Why Fawn?" Dan asked. "She's never been here before."

"She has a kind of . . . sixth sense, and a real gift for staying calm in situations like this."

Dan looked a little doubtful. "If you say so."

Dan grabbed three flashlights from the cupboard next to the dining table. He explained to Alex and Fawn that the three of them would be hiking toward the sky tower to look for Fee. "He'll be cold. We'll need to take some extra clothes."

Before leaving, they quickly sorted through the steaming jackets, gloves and hats draped near the fire. Each took an extra jacket, stuffed gloves and beanies in the pockets and tied them around their waists. Dan suggested they walk through the woods in a staggered pattern, making sure to stay in sight of each other's flashlights.

**

Fee was greatly relieved when Sonja and Dan gave him permission to start back. Finding the snowshoes at the bottom of the steps where he'd left them, he clipped them on and slipped downhill with no effort at all, a welcome reward for all the hard work it had taken to get to the sky tower. He was gliding along, lost in a daydream of sitting in front of the stove at the lodge, toasty and dry, when he began to sense a bit more friction, a bit less glide beneath his feet.

What the? – He stopped, took off his glasses and attempted to wipe them clean with his gloved hand. Even through the smudged surface he could see that the crunchy, glistening snow beyond was unblemished: no prints, no track, no walking stick holes. Where had he gone wrong?

Take stock, he told himself: he was going down-hill, the sun was on his left, so he was going in the right direction, there was (a little hesitation here) plenty of time ... besides the camp's outside lights would actually be easier to see if it got dark . . . as it was starting to do. The smoke from the wood stove in the lodge would be visible above the trees, a good guide as well. A tinge of panic shivered through him, nothing too debilitating, nothing he couldn't handle. Man, a hot shower will feel so great . . . or maybe he'd eat first, crawl into his sleeping bag after dinner and shower in the morning. Yeah, that's what he'd do.

But as twilight faded and the trees became ominous shapes against the snow, any chance of a long distance view was completely blocked. Had he drifted down a slope leading away from the lodge? The fear he'd so bravely kept at bay finally gripped his psyche, a colossal weight that eventually caused his knees to buckle. It seemed as if he'd traveled three times the distance it had taken to get to the sky tower; his body could no longer fight what seemed a losing battle. Exhausted, he crumpled to the frozen ground.

At first, a jolt of terror caused his throat to constrict and ache, but when he began to cry, the tears brought a welcome sense of relief. Plentiful and warm, they streamed down his cheeks in a soothing, calming gush of release. Accepting his fate was like a comforting arm around his shoulder; he leaned into it and closed his eyes. He thought of his mom and dad and sister and Grams and Gramps and his new friend, Nate – and went to sleep.

**

Dan's and Alex's flashlight beams were clearly visible to Fawn's left. She knew they were close to where the hill dropped off, so she edged further right. As she pushed through the snow, she called Fee's name, pausing often to listen for the slightest response, any tell-tale sound. After doing this numerous times her heart began to race and she wondered if she would hear anything above its pounding. It occurred to her that instead of pushing so hard, she could put her trust in the power of Source. Planting her feet, she lifted her left palm to the sky and rested her right hand on her belly. She focused on the crisp air flowing in and out of her lungs and all at once, she knew – Robert had found him.

She switched off her flashlight and was drawn further into the forest. In less than a minute, she came upon Robert kneeling over Fee. He had removed Fee's wet clothing and was struggling to put the barely conscious boy's legs into his own jacket. Fawn untied the extra jacket from her waist, and together the two managed to encase Fee's body in down. After Robert put his dry wool socks on the boy's feet, Fawn switched on her flashlight, put two fingers in her mouth, curled her tongue and blew. As she knew he would, Robert disappeared.

"She's got him!" Dan yelled. He and Alex rushed toward the piercing alarm and the sweeping beam of Fawn's flashlight.

The quiet kitchen was anything but calm. The group continued to make dinner, but their minds wandered from one unsettling thought to another. Would Fee be found? Would it be in time? What if he lived, but lost an extremity: a foot, a hand, a nose. Tears ran down Nate's cheeks; he blew his nose repeatedly. He and Fee had chosen the bottom bunks last night and laughed until Alex and Jeremy threatened to douse their beds in water if they didn't stop. With all his padding, Nate thought he could probably survive the cold – but Fee?

The acrid aroma of burning beans went unnoticed, a block of cheese sat partially grated on the counter. When Alisha dropped utensils on the floor, everyone jumped. June and Jeremy were chopping veggies when June noticed blood on a slice of onion and thought Jeremy had cut his finger – until she spotted a flap of flesh hanging from her thumb.

Jeremy shouted, "Bandage!" and Sonja, who had been pacing back and forth in her thwarted desire to *do something*, started searching for the first aid kit. But when she heard Fawn's distinctive whistle, she forgot the bloody thumb, grabbed a flashlight and bolted out the door. She had barely started up the hill when a figure came rushing toward her. "We need a stretcher," Alex called. "There's one behind the door in the men's bathroom at the end of the lodge.

"Go back," Sonja called. "I'll get it."

"You'll see our tracks take off to the right about twenty yards further up the trail. He was so close."

"Is he . . . ?" Sonja yelled, but Alex was gone.

By the time Sonja reached the group, they had rolled Fee in every available jacket. Alex and Dan lifted him onto the stretcher then teamed up at the front handholds; Sonja and Fawn took the back. Fawn struggled to lift her end high enough to match the level of her mother's grip.

When they reached the lodge they laid Fee in front of the stove. The other campers immediately surrounded him; Nate knelt on the floor at his side. "Should I rub his feet or something?"

"No," said Dan. "If tissue is frozen, rubbing can break it down."

"Nate?" Fee said, weakly.

"Right here," Nate said. "How do you feel?"

Sonja interrupted. "Nate, maybe Fee shouldn't be talking right now."

"Please let him stay," Fee croaked. "I'm so grateful. I really thought I was going to die."

One by one the dinner crew returned to the kitchen, all but Nate. Dan looked at the two boys. "Let's go help with dinner," he suggested to Sonja.

As soon as they were alone, Nate leaned in close. "Well?"

"I wasn't scared until it got really dark. That's when I realized I had no idea if I was headed in the right direction. When I finally gave up trying to get back, I just sat down and cried; actually, it made me feel better, then I went to sleep."

Fee hesitated for a moment. "I had the weirdest dream."

"Tell me before you forget," Nate whispered.

"This boy was pulling off my pants and forcing me to put my legs into a jacket. I told him I couldn't go to school like that, but he ignored me, like he couldn't even hear me. I wanted to fight him, but my arms and legs wouldn't move, and I kept saying everybody would tease me and begged him over and over to stop."

"Creepy."

"Way . . . Nate?"

"Huh?"

"Would you check my legs? They're starting to hurt a lot."

Nate lifted the layers of blanket and jackets to peek beneath. "Uh, Fee."

"Yeah"

"I can't really see them ...There's an upside down jacket on your legs."

"So somebody did do it."

"Yeah."

"Who found me?"

"Fawn."

"Oh, man . . . I'll never be able to look her in the eyes again."

CHAPTER 19

Fee's mishap had no serious ramifications. Dan notified his parents and offered to bring him home, but Fee assured them he was doing well, and they allowed him stay for the rest of the retreat. He avoided eye-contact with Fawn but sent an elaborate thank you note, passing it around before delivering it, so everyone would know he gave her full credit for saving his life.

Fawn did not fare so well. Her arms were sore from helping to carry Fee, but her back was excruciating. The only comfortable position she could find was flat on the floor with her legs resting on a chair. She was moved into Sonja's room. Everyone understood that the girl's counselor would take care of a female camper in distress, and they continued to pretend they weren't related. "I'm really glad you're here, Mom."

Sonja smoothed Fawn's tangled hair. "Me too."

"This back thing really sucks. I'm going to miss the New Year's Eve fireworks."

"I'm sure there's a way to make you comfortable outside."

"And," Fawn continued, "I'm worried about leaving. There won't be room in the van for me to lie down."

"I've been thinking about that," Sonja said. "Dan and I have been discussing the idea of you staying here."

Fawn perked up. "Really? I've been thinking about that too. I'd like to stay, and my sore back is the perfect excuse."

"Good. I can always drive up and bring you home if your back doesn't get better soon."

"I'll probably be fine in a few days. I had the same thing last Christmas. Remember?"

"That's right; you were lying on the floor in the living room when I put the lights on the tree." Sonja stared across the room. "Your dad had a back like yours. You both got sad when it happened to him because he couldn't pick you up."

"My gosh," said Fawn. "I think I remember that; I think I remember him lying on the floor."

"It was the only place he could get comfortable," Sonja said. "You slept next to him there more than once."

Fawn shrugged. "I don't really miss him, you know; it's been so long. But when you mention that kind of stuff, it feels hard somehow."

"I do know; sometimes it's still hard for me too." Sonja took her daughter's hand. "Well," she said gently, "let's talk more about you staying here."

"You'll need to mail some stuff to me, and change my home-school address."

"Of course."

Fawn looked out the window at the leafless oaks against a cloudless, blue sky. "Dan can teach Robert a lot," she said, "but he's too old to teach him to fit in. I think it's the job I was meant for from the beginning."

Sonja waited a moment, wondering if she should say what was on her mind. "Fawn?" Fawn looked into her mother's eyes; Sonja hesitantly aired her concern. "I don't want to harp, but I have to say it one more time ..."

Fawn interrupted. "No you don't," she said. "My behavior was inexcusable. You don't have to worry."

Fawn ended up on the same stretcher they had used for Fee, a little embarrassing, but kind of fun. Alex and Alisha teamed up with and Jeremy and June to carry her outside. They set the stretcher on a picnic table. Alex sat next to her to watch the fireworks so she wouldn't feel alone; it was awesome.

In the morning, the whole group helped shut up the kitchen and the cabins. When they were finished, Dan suggested they repeat the exercise they'd done on the platform so Fee could have the experience. The main room of the lodge was at least twice the length of the sky tower, but at least there was no snow to contend with. Fawn served as spotter, keeping an eye on the joined feet to make sure there were no gaps. Fee messed up on the first try, but they all held it together the second time, and the retreat ended on a perfect note.

Sonja was eager to get on the road. They would have to stop for lunch, and she was determined to reach the bay area before dark. As they were loading their walking sticks into the back, the group decided to keep track of future treks by carving one hash mark for any hike over four miles. This time, they filed into the van in an order they chose themselves: the girls sat together in the far back, Nate, Fee and Jeremy in the middle seat, and Alex up front. They rolled out just after 10:00 a.m.

**

Fawn was in bed when the van drove away. She felt her decision to stay was the right one, and yet, she felt hollow, and a little anxious. Writing to Isabelle helped settle her thoughts:

> January 1, 2013
>
> Dear Grandmother,
> When I left your house to come to Muir Camp with Mom and the other kids I thought I might end up going home and starting school next week, but I never imagined I would be writing to you to say I won't be leaving Muir Camp. Somehow, though, I think you may not be surprised when I tell you I am staying to help Robert learn how to fit in with his modern day peers. (as if I'm some kind of pro – Ha! Ha !)
> My time with you changed everything. I love you so much and I will keep my promise to discuss with you any decision regarding my gift.
> You are so special to me,
> Fawn
>
> P.S. Write if you have time. It's just me and the guys here. I can always use your advice and would like to hear how things are going there.
> P.S.S. I promise to finish my basket next time I come to the farm.

P.S.S.S. I get to have the room Mom had during the retreat. It is right off of the kitchen and really sunny. I'm going to start plants from seeds on my window sill and plant a garden.

Fawn had just finished the letter when she heard a knock on her door. "Hello," she called.

Dan opened the door. "Mind if I come in?"

"Not at all," Fawn said. "I was just writing a letter to my grandmother."

Dan crossed the room and sat near the window. "Does she still live in San Diego?"

"That's my mom's mom. I'm writing to my dad's mother. She lives in Los Padres National Forest . . . near Fort Liggett if you know where that is."

"I do. You and your mom live in Paso Robles, right?"

"Uh huh. Before my dad died we lived at my grandmother's farm, but when I got older Mom wanted us to live near a school. I've actually been staying at the farm for the last four months. I'm already doing home schooling, so it will be easy to continue that while I'm here."

"Your mom told me about that." Dan got up and moved toward the door. His expression, it seemed to Fawn, had shifted from friendly to . . . what? . . . concerned. "Well, let me know if there's anything I can get for you; there's a call button right there. It's a way for the interns and cooks to reach me during camping season; everything is so spread out here. I'll be back later and bring you some dinner."

"I'm looking forward to meeting Robert," Fawn said.

"It won't be long. He probably knows you didn't leave with the others." Dan stretched his arms over his head. "I think I'll go lie down for a while, too."

Dan was of two minds about the decision to have Fawn stay at the camp. No doubt he could use the help. He'd told Sonja several times he was worried about the socialization aspect of Robert's education. But now that she was staying, he had to admit he felt a little possessive of the boy – and he had questions; why had Fawn been living with her grandmother? Was she a troublemaker? Surely, Sonja wouldn't set him up for that. He sighed; had he just been roped into being the foster parent of not one, but two?

**

A few hours later, Fawn heard another knock at her door, but when she called 'come in,' it was Robert, not Dan, who presented the dinner tray. The two looked straight into the other's eyes until Fawn turned toward the bedside table to clear a place to set the tray. The twist was a mistake, and she let out a screech of pain. Robert's eyes widened. He hurried to set the tray on the nightstand, then started for the door.

Fawn caught her breath and, with Herculean effort, calmly asked him to stay. "It's just my back," she assured him. "I hurt it the other night. It has nothing to do with you."

"You carry . . . weak boy."

Relieved that he understood, and a little nervous, Fawn began to chatter. "That was so scary – Fee could have died – You saved his life – I didn't know if you knew it was me out there – It was so dark, and you didn't really seem to look at me, and . . ."

"Enough," Robert said forcefully. He walked to the

other side of the room, sat down on the floor and stared out the window.

Fawn was thoroughly humiliated. What an idiot; four months of training in the wisdom of silence and she'd gushed words like a broken sewer pipe. She sat back in bed and forced herself to eat her dinner slowly.

Robert never so much as glanced her way while she was eating, but the moment she was done he picked up the tray. "Good-bye," he said. "See you to-mor-row."

Embarrassing as it was, Fawn had to use the intercom to ask for Dan's help. He arrived in a flash and, without hesitation, picked her up, carried her into the bathroom, put her in a stall, and then waited in the hallway until she called him to carry her back to bed. A little red-faced, she thanked him profusely; he quickly shifted the subject Robert's visit.

"It was okay," she said. "His language skills aren't great, and I started talking too much; he had no trouble calling me on it . . . talk about embarrassed."

"Enough?"

"You guessed it. I heard you tell Mom it was his first word . . . blunt, and effective. I don't know if he'll ever want to see me again. Did he say anything to you?"

"No. He didn't come back to the cottage. I was hoping he'd want to talk about the weekend, but I guess he isn't ready, or maybe he has nothing to say."

"I've tried to put myself in his shoes," Fawn said. "Then it occurred to me I would have to look at it as putting myself in his bare feet. It's a whole different dimension."

Dan sighed. "I have to remind myself of that all the time."

"Thanks for letting me stay. For years I've dreamt about meeting Robert, wondering what my part in *The Plan* would be. I see now that no one really knows what comes next."

"In my own way, I feel close to him," Dan said, "but I'm not sure it's reciprocal. It's his unflinching stare that gets to me, not exactly disconnected, but . . . "

"Lonely?"

Dan nodded. "Maybe that's it."

Fawn gazed out the window at the moon shadows on the frozen landscape. "I hope he'll let me be his friend."

CHAPTER 20

On the return to San Francisco, Alex slumped in the front seat of the van under a cloud of disillusionment, disappointment, depression. He had counted the days until he would return to Muir Camp, was buoyed by Dan's request that he prepare to put on chains if need be and had, if he were honest, envisioned himself in a leadership role.

He'd shot up in the past four months, was just two inches short of six feet, athletic, a four-point-o and, at least amongst his peers, accustomed to being literally, and figuratively, looked up to. Instead, he totally blew it when he tried to lead a group exercise, not to mention Alisha's eye to eye confrontation and her accusation that he thought he was 'the big man here.' Top that off with the wimpiest of the group getting tons of attention after the unbelievably stupid move of missing the only trail back to the lodge and nearly freezing to death. Alex was majorly irritated, and the really irritating part was he couldn't justify his irritation.

Sonja glanced over at him. "Hey, you're pretty quiet over there."

"Yes," Alex replied. Wanting to move the conversation in a different direction he asked, "When do you think Fawn will be ready to go home?"

"I don't know. Apparently she's had this problem before. The choice for her to stay was probably wise."

"That girl sure has a hell of a whistle . . . Excuse me, a heck of a whistle."

Sonja laughed. "Yes, she does."

"I think she said she lives with her grandmother."

Sonja kept her eyes on the road. "That's where I picked her up."

Alex looked out the window at acres of orchard, the occasional farmhouse and barn. "I wish I had grandparents to live with."

"All of your grandparents have passed away?"

"Yes. Both of my parents were born when their parents were in their forties, and I was born when my parents were in their thirties. None of my grandparents made it much past seventy, so I missed out."

"Me too," Sonja said, glad to have found some common ground. "My mom's mom was still alive when I was born. I was named after her, but she lived in Norway; we never met. My dad's folks passed on when he was just ten, auto accident. His aunt and uncle gave him a home until he turned eighteen. All kinds of ways to grow up, I guess."

"Uh-huh."

A small valley town was just ahead; Sonja called to the group, "You guys ready to stop for lunch?" The response was a resounding yes.

Phone calls made during the lunch stop gave parents

plenty of time to get to the Ferry Building. When they arrived, everyone scrambled out of the van, grabbed their gear and walking sticks, and were headed home within ten minutes – everyone but Alex.

"Want me to drop you off at your house?" Sonja asked.

"No thanks, my parents will be here soon. I like hanging out at the water front; there's always lots of street musicians around."

"I'm responsible for you until your parents come. Let's give them a call."

"I'm fine, really," Alex said.

"I know you are, but it's my job. Sorry."

Alex looked at his phone. "Oh, man, my battery is dead."

Sonja pulled her cell out of her pocket. "Give me the number."

Alex sighed; no way out of this one. He recited the number and held his breath.

"This is Sonja Henderson. I'm at the ferry building with Alex. I was just wondering if one of his parents is on the way to pick him up."

Alex knew his parents were going to spend New Year's Eve at their cottage on the Russian River. Lucia must have answered the phone, but Lucia didn't have a car. He knew what was coming.

"I'll be glad to," he heard Sonja say. "We'll be there in a few minutes."

Alex gave Sonja directions. He'd considered having her drop him off in front of an apartment building in North Beach, but he was sure she wouldn't fall for it, would want to see him walk through a door, delivered safe and sound.

It was obvious Lucia had been watching for them. When they pulled up in front of the house, the gate opened and Sonja drove through. Dressed in her white uniform (Alex suspected she'd had her regular clothes on before Sonja called), Lucia approached the van with a big smile and thanked Sonja profusely for bringing her 'Master Alex' home.

"My pleasure," Sonja told her.

"Would you like to come in for some refreshment," Lucia offered.

One look at Alex's face told Sonja she should decline. "That's so generous of you," she said, "but I still have quite a drive in front of me."

As the van backed out of the drive, Alex waved goodbye and called "Thanks for the ride," then he handed his small duffel to Lucia and headed for the house. When the front door closed, Lucia took the brunt of Alex's frustration. "Damn it, Lucia, don't you ever do that again."

"What are you . . . ?"

"I've asked nicely before," Alex shouted.

His face was flushed, but his eyes were cold. It struck Lucia how much he looked like his father; she glanced away.

"Look at me," Alex ordered. "The word master comes out of your mouth one more time, and I will find a way to get you fired." For a nanosecond he thought she was going to light right back into him, but her face crumpled as if she was about to cry. He turned his back on her, stormed upstairs to his room and slammed the door.

When his parents arrived later that evening, Lucia told them she was getting the flu and needed to spend a few days at her daughter's house. She left that night, and she never

came back. Alex had broken the heart of his greatest ally –
and he wasn't sure he cared.

**

Robert laid in the sweat lodge under Buck's skin. He'd
been thinking about the girl who stayed, Fawn, the one who
had found him helping the boy who slept in the snow and
brought the others running with her shrill call. Dan had told
him the adult female with the group was the girl's mother;
surprising, they looked nothing alike. But what was truly
unexpected was to learn that Sonja was the human that
Condor had communicated with all these years, the human
who had helped The Council with The Plan! How could it
be that Sonja could enter the sacred space of silent communication with Condor, and yet it was Fawn who somehow
signaled kin?

Questioning – Confusion – Enough! No more warm
cottage, shoes, or layers of second skin; he would not allow
himself to become a weak one. He threw off Buck's hide,
stood up and, wearing only the shorts, set off to run.

**

Fawn simply could not hold it any longer, but it was
four in the morning. She couldn't bring herself to pick up the
intercom and wake up Dan while it was still dark. Rolling
out of bed onto the floor, she began to crawl toward the door.

The height of the door knob was formidable. She
reached with her right arm; the pain was so sharp it took her
breath away. After waiting a moment she tried her left,
stretching as far as she could, then a tad more, and POP! The
searing discomfort lessened. She reached again, pop, pop,

161

pop in quick succession – ahhhh. With the help of a nearby chair, she pulled herself to standing and shuffled to the bathroom. By the time Dan entered with the breakfast tray, she was sitting at the table by the window.

"Hey, you're up," he said. "Your face looks completely different without that furrowed brow you've been wearing for the last few days."

"I'm healed!" said Fawn. "I was crawling to the bathroom, and when I reached for the door knob, my spine popped back into place. I'm still a little shaky, but much, much better."

"Look!" Dan said, pointing out the window. "There he goes."

Fawn turned to see Robert sprint across a snowy slope, wearing nothing but shorts. "Wow," she laughed "and I thought I was tough."

That evening, using her walking stick for support, Fawn gingerly made her way to Dan's cottage for an early supper. "Do you think he'll come?" she asked.

"I don't know," Dan said. "I don't try to predict, or worry too much either."

"Mom says we're like hot-house flowers, that Aborigines can withstand freezing temperatures. Imagine if I'd been alone outside when my back messed up . . . or if we hadn't found Fee."

Dan opened the wood stove's heavy steel door and tossed a fresh log on the glowing coals. "The problem with us modern humans," he mused, "is, unlike sprinting through the snow half-naked, our habits don't *appear* to be life threatening. We exploit the planet in pursuit of comfort through excess with hardly a thought of the consequences."

Fawn shook her head; her brow furrowed with conflicting thoughts. "Can The Council's plan possibly work?"

Dan sighed. "I don't know, but I'm glad to be part of the effort."

"Me, too," said Fawn.

Dan had left the stove door open, and they both stared at the crackling flames. A squeak from the bathroom door hinge interrupted their contemplations.

Robert had arrived.

**

The boy had become accustomed to entering Dan's cottage through the bathroom window so if he changed his mind, he could easily slip away. He'd seen the girl walk to the cottage; his desire to learn the powerful two-fingered sound was the reason for his visit. After climbing through the window, a casual glance as he passed the bathroom mirror stopped him in his tracks.

He'd looked into the mirror many times, comparing his reflection to the photos of young people in the book called catalog: their facial expressions, their clothes, the way they held their bodies. What struck him now was the recognition that what had signaled Fawn as kin were the physical characteristics they shared: high cheekbones, dark eyes, black hair, shape of mouth, one slightly protruding ear.

Until a few days ago, the boy had not considered that humans, like birds, had not only profoundly different appearances, but that those appearances might signal different families of the same species. He'd contemplated the heron, its nest of sticks big enough for him to lie down in, and the tiny yellow bird whose nest of grasses was no bigger than his palm.

Opening the bathroom door, he walked straight toward the girl, extended his hand and led her to the mirror. Side by side they peered at the reflection. "What are you?" the boy asked.

"I'm a girl; I am Fawn."

He shook his head. "No."

"Yes, Fawn is my name, like your name is Robert."

"No. Telele."

"What?"

"My name, Telele." The boy had no words to explain how he had found his human name, no words to describe his suspicion that both of them were connected to the ethereal family who had given him his name. He looked deep into her eyes; there was something familiar, a dim memory. He could almost . . .

**

Fawn looked away from Robert's prying gaze. Did he suspect she was the fawn who blocked his path in the ravine, the one who slept next to him the night before he met Dan? Was that what he was implying when he said, "What are you?"

CHAPTER 21

Evenings found Dan and Fawn in the cottage, Fawn at home schooling tasks, Dan on the computer or reading. At first they both held an expectation that Robert would appear, but his visits were sporadic at best. He continued to sleep in the sweat lodge, wear his original shorts and forage for food.

Fawn took every opportunity to interact with Robert, careful to check any mindless babble. She read to him, as often as he would sit still and listen, and his vocabulary continued to improve. Soon he began to formulate questions: *Fawn, Telele, same family?* Maybe. *Who protects family, who grows children?* Fawn tried to explain how in times past those responsibilities were similar to the creatures who raised him but, in many modern human cultures, men's and women's roles were more fluid, one had choices.

The onset of spring brought them closer. Fawn often gathered basket-making materials near the place where Robert had been given his true name. He enjoyed watching her weave the plants into a container he would have called box, but was corrected to say 'basket.' Robert had learned a myriad of names for the things he encountered at the camp, but had not contemplated how those things had come to be. When he heard Dan say, "Fawn, that's beautiful," he began to examine that word. Like 'job' or 'work,' 'beautiful' was not a thing, not a color, or function, or movement, but he sensed the word somehow spoke of gratitude.

As temperatures warmed, he and Fawn explored further from camp. Fawn often used the word beautiful to describe things that were ordinary to Robert: a field in blossom, bright green moss clinging to granite, a cascading waterfall. He began to see in a different way, began to notice the beauty of his first 'friend.'

**

Even though Fawn's influence had accelerated Robert's development, Dan had strong reservations as to whether the boy would be ready to interact with his peers by summer. He expressed his doubts to Sonja. "He's a long way from passing as a twenty-first century kid."

"I've been thinking about that, too," Sonja said. "He trusts Fawn, right?"

"He does . . . much more than me."

"How about I come up in a couple of weeks and bring both of them to my house," Sonja offered.

Dan looked around the cabin, his eyes drawn to Robert's jacket hanging on the peg by the door. "I don't know."

Sonja pressed. "No doubt it would be a shock for Robert to come to Paso Robles, but I think we can agree that the best method for adaptation is immersion . . . it's only four months until the start of the boy's session at Muir Camp."

"You really think he could be ready?" Dan asked.

"I think this could be our best shot." Silence. "Dan?"

"I . . . " Dan cleared his throat. "I thought I could pull it off, you know?"

"Dan, you have pulled it off; just think of the progress he's made. It's time for me to step up to the plate, time for you to take a break. Once he's here, P3 may have permission to communicate with him again, too. That would be really helpful."

Dan knew Sonja was right, but the idea of Robert leaving Muir Camp gave him a feeling of almost unbearable emptiness. What, at times, he thought would never end was about to; it hit him like a ton of bricks. The impact was so much more than he'd ever imagined, it was difficult for him to speak. Through an aching throat he asked, "Do you want to talk to Fawn? She and Robert are just outside the door."

"I would," Sonja said. "She'll have to be on board for this, too."

Dan sighed. "I can guarantee you don't have to worry about that."

**

Fawn sat in her sunny room at Muir Camp admiring the flourishing garden outside the window. She remembered how amused Robert had been when the three of them put up a deer fence with extra screen near the bottom to keep rabbits from destroying the little crop of vegetables. Soon they would be leaving all of this. It made her more than a little sad.

The bundle of reeds and grasses she'd harvested for baskets would come with her, and yet she couldn't imagine weaving at the modern little house in Paso Robles. Even though home-schooling had gone well, Sonja thought it best for Fawn to finish the year with her class, and homework would not include basketry.

A tutor had already been arranged for Robert – "someone who does this professionally." It made perfect sense, but what, Fawn wondered, would happen to Telele? Robert spoke often of the village and the people he saw in a misty haze who gave him his true name. But 'Telele' could not co-exist with the modern human Robert was to become, not, at least, until 'Robert' was fully developed.

When she thought on these things, the wisdom of the entire Plan became questionable in Fawn's mind, and yet her life had become all the more unique and enriched by The Council's decision. For the first time, she had a peer she felt really close to, was totally comfortable with. Who knew, maybe one day when they were older . . .

CHAPTER 22

Dan talked Sonja into letting him do the driving. After all, she was busy, and he hadn't been on a road trip for quite a while. They would take 'Old Blue' into town and rent a comfortable car for the long drive.

He knew Sonja was right; leaving Muir Camp would force Robert to adapt. He would have to wear shoes, have to sleep inside, have to eat what was put in front of him. Dan would miss him, would miss Fawn as well. And to think, at one time he was worried about being stuck with those two; now he wondered what he would do without them.

It was early morning when Dan and Robert slid the barn doors open. Dan thought about the night of the caged raccoons; some kind of change happened that night, a change he couldn't exactly put his finger on. But there were plenty of changes he could put his finger on. The wild boy wore clothes, could express himself and understood much of what he heard. He used utensils and tools, had organized an entire barn, repaired two types of roof, stacked a winter's worth of wood, had oiled and painted and cleaned.

Dan reconnected the battery of the old truck and rolled it out. Glancing in the rear view mirror, he saw Robert taking a visual inventory then disappear into the barn for a few seconds before closing the doors. "See something out of place?" he asked.

"Yes," said Robert.

"What?"

"Orange cord."

Dan had thrown the heavy extension cord into the corner instead of hanging it on the wall. "Thank you," he said.

"Welcome," Robert replied.

Politeness, too, Dan thought.

Fawn was waiting at the front of the lodge. They loaded her few belongings into the bed of the truck, then pulled up in front of the cottage to load Robert's small chest of drawers and the duffel Dan had packed for himself. On the way out, Robert asked Dan to stop near the sweat lodge. He jumped out of the vehicle, returned with Buck's remains and put them in the back. Dan hadn't favored Robert taking Buck, but he didn't comment. It was really the only thing, other than the 'blue second-skin', the boy knew to be his own.

The three of them were comfortable on the spacious bench seat. Fawn happily sat in the middle as they rocked down the gravel road, past the meadow and onto the pavement, headed for civilization.

Once they reached the outskirts of town, Robert swung his head left then right, then out the back window as if he could not believe what he had just seen. When they encountered a yellow school bus, jammed with students, his gawking was so obvious, kids began to wave and press their faces against the glass, grossly distorting their features. Robert grimaced; Fawn took his hand. "They're just playing," she said. "They mean no harm."

Robert was quiet for a moment. "Face False," he said. Fawn's brows pulled together. "Hmmmm, I guess that's one way to put it."

When they reached the rental car lot, Dan parked the truck off to the side and suggested Fawn and Robert unload the back while he secured the car. Everything was waiting in a pile when Dan pulled up in a white economy sedan. Robert's small chest of drawers and Dan's duffel filled the trunk. Everything else, and one passenger, would have to fit into the back seat. They crammed it all on one side with Buck on top of the pile; much to Fawn's relief, Robert slid into the back.

The travelers were quiet as they headed out of town. Looking for diversion, Dan decided to see what he could find on the radio; the first thing that came over the airwaves was the rant of an angry man.

"Why is man growling?" Robert asked.

Dan thought about the question. "It's his job."

Robert was intrigued. "His job to be afraid?"

"He's not afraid," Dan said. "It's his job to make other people afraid."

"Enough," said Robert.

When Dan turned off the radio, Fawn looked over and smiled. "I like his limits," she said.

Dan nodded. "I'm glad he has them. Do you think he'll be … oh, never mind. Let's just say, I'm really glad you two have become friends."

"Me too," Fawn agreed. "I can't believe it sometimes. I've known about all of this for years, at first just overhearing my mom and dad talk, and then Mom keeping me updated whenever she heard from P3. It's been so much a part of my life, I guess I'd forgotten how strange it actually is. W-Y-R-D, you know what I mean?"

"Your mom told me about that the first time we talked."

"Fate, destiny," Fawn said, "and here we all are, even Buck."

A whisper from the back seat . . . "Even Buck."

They were on the outskirts of Fresno, a sprawling city in the center of the San Joaquin Valley. Dan was lost in his thoughts; Fawn had fallen asleep. Robert draped his arm protectively around Buck as moving dens, big as buildings, hurtled along dangerously close to the car. His angst was exacerbated by the pressure building in his bladder. He had never learned the word for what he needed to do.

"Dan!" Robert yelled.

Dan's heart jumped, Fawn bolted upright.

"What?"

"Stop! . . . Here!"

"I can't just . . . " Dan began.

"NOW!" Robert searched for an association. "BATH-ROOM!"

Dan swung to the side of the road, and the boy bolted out of the car to relieve himself, completely oblivious of any need for subtlety. There were honks and hoots. Humiliated, Fawn kept her eyes down and began to chastise Dan. "I can't believe you haven't clued Robert in about plumbing," she said. "I mean really, Dan, this is basic stuff, you know ... like more basic than repairing roofs. Jeez."

"The only bathroom behavior he was interested in was a hot shower," Dan said. "As for the rest of it, he was put off, so I let it go. He *had* the whole outdoors." Dan's defensiveness suddenly mellowed into a shy cajolery. "When you get home, maybe you could . . . "

"Dan, I'm a thirteen-year-old female."

"You're right. We're going to stop to eat soon. I'll take him to the restroom, and we'll have a man to man about elimination options."

They stopped for Mexican fast food. Dan figured beans, rice and salad would work okay for Robert, and the restroom would, most likely, be clean.

"I'll order while you and Robert wash your hands," Fawn said.

"Good idea," Dan agreed. "Follow me, Robert."

As soon as they stepped through the door Dan walked up to the urinal; Robert watched like a boy learning from his father. When he looked into the small metal space that held the toilet, he understood he had to accept its use. Dan squirted a dab of soap in his palm and washed his hands; Robert rinsed his hands, but steered clear of the pink, scented liquid.

When they returned to the table, Robert slid in close to Fawn. His legs were shaking, and she could hear him inhaling deeply. Acknowledging his discomfort, she said, "Traveling is stressful."

Robert thought of the raccoons, the hissing mother and her frightened babies. "Car is cage," he said.

"**The** car is **a** cage," Fawn corrected, hoping the lesson would give Robert something else to think about. "It's okay," she said." You'll feel better when we get to my house. I promise."

Sonja's house was at the end of a cul-de-sac. She had chosen it for the location; the lots were big, the houses small, and the neighborhood was surrounded by large tracts of empty land. When they got out of the car, Robert looked beyond the houses toward the expanse of rolling hills and said, "Beautiful."

Sonja hurried out to greet them. "Mom," Fawn shouted, and ran into Sonja's open arms. Sonja looked over her daughter's head at Dan. "Welcome, how was the trip?"

"Good," Dan replied. "I haven't been down this way in years."

"I bet you guys are hungry; dinner's ready. Let's eat, then we'll bring the stuff in from the car." Fawn and Robert raced ahead. As Sonja and Dan walked toward the house, she glanced at the packed vehicle and whispered, "Does the big boy in the backseat smell?"

"Not really," Dan said, "Sorry, I just couldn't say no."

"It's okay. I've cleaned out my office; Robert will have his own space. It's up to him what he has in there."

Dan put his arm around Sonja. "You're a peach, you know that?"

"I've been called lots of things, but never a peach; I think I like it."

The dinner conversation focused on the immediate future. Fawn would start school in three days. Robert's tutor had been secured and would be working with him five days a week.

Sonja turned to Robert. "The tutor will teach you language skills, reading and math. You'll learn about money and shopping, all kinds of practical things."

Robert listened attentively. The changes he was about to experience were starting to sink in. He would have a new teacher called tutor. Dan would be going back to Muir Camp without him; the thought made it difficult for him to swallow.

"How much does the tutor know about Robert?" Dan asked.

"I told him a boy from Mexico would be coming to live with me, that he was born deaf, and a church group brought him to the U. S. for surgery to correct the problem. I said the surgery was successful, that the boy was very intelligent, but was, naturally, underdeveloped in terms of language and social skills. Voila," Sonja said with a flourish.

As her words tumbled out, Robert reasoned Sonja was talking about him. He knew the word deaf; he and Dan had experimented with some sign language after the flat hand signal became part of their vocabulary. The word surgery he'd learned from Fawn, who used it while removing a splinter from his finger with needle and tweezers when they built the garden fence.

The rest of the group was chatting amiably when the boy interjected a statement that stopped the conversation cold. "Sonja speak false."

Sonja blushed. "Where did you hear those words, Robert?"

"Condor," the boy answerered. "Speak false like bird drag wing . . . decoy. You protect nest."

A wave of relief washed over Sonja. "Yes," she said, "That's right."

Robert spent the rest of the evening in his new room. Sonja had moved a futon in from the living room to serve as a bed, but Dan assured her the boy would prefer the floor, so the two of them returned to its original spot.

"He's a hard surface sleeper," said Dan.

Sonja shook her head. "Isn't it strange how we just assume what makes us comfortable would make anyone comfortable."

"I remember hearing the phrase, assumption is a dirty word," Dan said. "It's something to contemplate."

"Yes," Sonja agreed. "Yes it is."

CHAPTER 23

"My name is Alan Chu."

When the knock came at precisely 9:00 a.m., Robert was ready to answer the door. He stuck out his hand and said, "I am Roberto Muniz." He and Sonja had rehearsed this self-introduction several times. Reciting a list of surnames, she'd let Robert decide which one to adopt; Muniz rolled off his tongue easily.

"Roberto Muniz is the name you will use from now on," she'd explained. "It is part of the decoy." He had introduced himself perfectly. Now Sonja stepped forward. "Nice to see you again, Alan. I'm glad you were able to arrange your schedule to accommodate ours."

Alan was all smiles and enthusiasm. "This is a perfect practicum for me. My professor has already cleared it."

"Great. So, five mornings a week, correct?"

"Nine to one, that's my plan," Alan said. "I especially like the idea of Roberto and I having lunch together."

"Good. There may be days you want to eat out; just let me know and I'll give Roberto money. Mexican food is his favorite, of course. If you want to go to the beach or take a hike, we'll pack a sack lunch."

"The park could be nice, too," Alan added. "There are tennis courts there; I could teach him to play. I have an extra racket."

**

Robert was too distracted to understand any of the conversation between Tutor and Sonja. He knew Tutor had introduced himself with a different name, but he'd been so preoccupied with pronouncing his own, he couldn't remember what Tutor said.

"Are you two ready to get to work?" Sonja asked.

Work – Robert knew that word well. Did this house need roof repair?

Tutor held up a canvas bag. "I've got all my tools right here."

"I'm on my way then," said Sonja. "You have my cell if you need anything." She put her arm around Robert and squeezed; he did his best not to stiffen.

Tutor spread the contents of his bag on the kitchen table. "Roberto, come sit here with me."

Robert pulled out a chair, sat down and eyed the *tools* in front of him. He had seen books and pencils, but Dan's desk had not been of particular interest.

"We will begin by learning the alphabet. Can you say alphabet?"

"Alphabet."

Tutor set a piece of paper in front of each of them and handed Robert a pencil. "Here we go," he said. "Letter number one, A." He made marks on the paper and pointed to each one saying, "Capitol A, lower case a. Now you, try."

Robert labored to make the same marks and sounds.

"Ah, left handed." Tutor repositioned the pencil in Robert's fingers and the boy tried again.

The work went on for a very long time. Robert did not like this kind of work.

**

It was nearly dark when Sonja walked through the door. Fawn and Robert were in the kitchen, Fawn happily giving orders, Robert happily following them.

"Smells good in here," Sonja said. "What are you guys making?"

"Spaghetti and salad," Fawn replied.

Robert was stuffing his mouth with the mushrooms, carrots, and cucumber he'd been slicing. He and Alan hadn't had lunch today. Alan, in fact, had left early.

"So, how was the tutor?" Sonja asked.

"Tutor . . . name." said Robert.

"Alan."

"Alan," Robert echoed. "Alan, Alan."

"I don't think Alan knew what he was getting into," Fawn said. "Tomorrow might be better though. I took Robert up to the 'No Trespassing' sign on the other side of the field. He's starting to understand why knowing how to read is important."

Robert sliced a carrot round then whacked off two edges at a slant. "Capitol A," he said.

"More than one way to skin a cat," Fawn trilled. She smiled at her mom whom she'd often teased for using old phrases like that one. Sonja raised her eyebrows and returned the grin.

"Skin a cat?" Robert said.

"One of these days," Fawn laughed, "I'll explain idioms. Mom knows lots of them."

Alan called after dinner to tell Sonja he wanted Robert to have a bag lunch the next day. "I think we're just going to play tomorrow. I need some time to research different ways to engage Roberto in studying academics." Sonja shared Fawn's idea of making letters out of vegetables.

"Hey," Alan said, "I can use all the help I can get."

The next day Robert and Alan went into town. They used the bus service to get around and went to the park to play tennis. Robert learned several new words; public, transportation, net, ball, racket, bounce, chocolate. Chocolate was a very popular word with Roberto. He repeated it numerous times, each repetition rewarded with another piece, until Alan said, "That's enough," and was pleased when Robert laughed.

Fawn dedicated herself to teaching Robert the alphabet. They spent time in the field behind the house using sticks to draw letters in the dirt. Fawn recalled a technique one of her elementary school teachers had used. When they got to the letter C she made a drawing of a cat in the shape of a C to associate the sound with the letter. Before long she enlisted help from students in her art class.

With the teacher's support, Fawn told the story of how "Roberto" had come to live in the United States and 'Teaching Roberto His Letters' became an art class project. In no time Robert's ceiling was plastered with drawings: a B shaped Bumble Bee, M shaped Mountains, a Slithery S shaped Snake.

Extra points were given for difficult letters and for incorporating the lower case version of the letter somewhere in the drawing. Dan had given Robert a flashlight as a going-away gift, and every night before going to sleep he focused the light on each one, admiring the details, memorizing its shape and the sound that went with it.

Alan's idea to play tennis was a bright spot in Robert's education. Although they never kept score, it wasn't long before the boy could easily have beaten his tutor. Math and money were a different story. There were coins and paper and tickets and passes and credit cards, all kinds of ways to 'buy.' And behind all that was numbers.

"Maybe numbers are going to have to wait," Sonja said. She and Alan were sitting on a park bench while Robert and Fawn played on a jungle gym like kids half their age.

"Well, what's the plan?" Alan asked. "Are you going to try to enroll him in school next year?"

"I don't know; we're taking it a day at a time. I think the fact that he's feeling comfortable in public, and can make himself understood, is encouraging.

"I've been talking to Fawn about organizing a little party for the kids who participated in the letter drawing project," Alan said. "One thing Roberto has not had is much contact with a group of people his own age."

When Fawn and Robert flopped down on the grass in front of the bench, the party became the topic of conversation.

"What do you think, Fawn? Want to throw a party?" Alan asked.

"Party?" Robert said. He had never heard the word, but he knew the word throw.

"A party," Sonja began, "is a group of people having fun."

Robert tried to sort out what he thought he heard. "People throw things?" he asked.

The question struck Fawn as hilarious. Each time she tried to come up with an explanation for the phrase she doubled over again, imagining the endless things that might be thrown at a party, or the entire gathering being swept up and hurled into space, circling the planet like a lopsided moon.

"Throw a party is an expression," Sonja said, seriously. "What we call a figure of speech."

"Here's the deal," Fawn explained. "The person or people who "throw" (she emphasized the word by making little quotation marks with her fingers) a party, get to decide where the party will be, what kinds of things we will do, and what we will eat."

"Chocolate," said Robert.

The party was set for a Saturday morning in late May at a nearby lake: picnic lunch, volleyball, and swimming if the water wasn't too cold. Fawn, Alan and Robert shopped for party favors, and Fawn made a basket as a special prize for Robert's favorite drawing.

When the day finally arrived, Robert was obviously nervous; he paced, he fidgeted. When he walked into his room, Sonja said to Fawn, "He's driving me nuts."

"He's worried, Mom." Fawn knocked on Robert's door. "Can I come in?"

"Yes."

Robert stood in front of a mirror combing his hair. He was wearing a light blue Tee shirt with a picture of a monkey on the front. Other shirts were strewn on the floor.

"Animal," Robert said, pointing to his shirt. "Word."

"Monkey," Fawn replied.

"Monkey shirt okay?"

"Yes, and don't forget, you'll want an extra pair of shorts for swimming."

Robert opened a drawer and started analyzing each pair of shorts. Fawn reached around him, grabbed a pair and closed the drawer. "These will work fine," she said. "You look great. We're going to have fun."

"Tennis is fun," he countered.

"This will be, too."

Sonja had rented two vans. Alan drove one, she drove the other. They managed to squeeze in eighteen kids along with a few blow-up rafts, a volley ball set, two ice chests full of food and a cake with "Roberto's Teaching Team" written in frosting.

The cake was chocolate.

Robert rode up front in Sonja's van and stared straight ahead while other kids carried on noisy conversations. Sonja could see his jaw muscles tightening. "Hold it down back there," Sonja called. "I'm having a hard time concentrating on my driving." The decibel level dropped a bit. When they arrived at the lake, Robert waited until the others were far from the van before he made his exit.

"Are you okay?" Fawn asked.

"Enough," he said.

"Kids these days are noisy. You'll get used to it."

"I stay in van," Robert said.

"I **will** stay in **the** van," Fawn reminded him. "But you won't, because I could use some help setting up the food table. Come on."

After the table was set, Fawn wandered off to join a group of girls nearby. Robert felt adrift, adrift in a sea of noise. The motors of several small aluminum boats were barely muffled enough to keep him from quaking; a thumping bass line from down the beach, set him on edge. He needed another job. He glanced toward Fawn, hoping she would look his way and give him some direction. But it was Sonja who attempted to come to his rescue.

"See Barry over there?" Sonja pointed to one of the boys alone on the dock. "I'll give you some money and you can invite him to take a paddle boat ride with you." Robert looked doubtful; Sonja pressed. "Robert this is skill building, an opportunity for interaction. This is how a person makes friends."

"I have friends," Robert said firmly. "Fawn, Alan, Dan … you."

"You have a duty, young man," Sonja said, sternly. She regretted her words, and the tone in her voice when she delivered them, as soon as they came out of her mouth.

Robert stood still and silently stared past Sonja.

Fawn started to feel uneasy. She turned her attention away from the knot of girls and looked to see if Robert was still at the food table. What she saw was a light blue tee-shirt rapidly disappearing on the trail that circled the lake, and her mother was walking toward her. Even from a distance, the tight lips, squinted eyes, and Sonja's *I am so pissed off* walk, left no doubt that something was wrong. She stepped away from the group and walked toward Sonja. "What's up?" she said. Sonja had simply waved off Fawn's inquiry and kept right on going. "Mom?"

Without missing a step, Sonja said, "He'll be back."

And he was, just as the group gathered to eat.

Robert walked over to the end of a line that had formed for the luncheon buffet. After dishing up a plate, he took a seat at the far end of the table, kept his head down and concentrated on his food. When they'd finished eating, Alan took the part of Master of Ceremonies. He directed each artist to find the laminated copy of their drawing and sit back down. "When it's your turn," he said, "I'd like for you to stand, introduce yourself to Roberto and describe your work."

With each introduction, Robert looked directly at the artist, doing his best to understand what they said. He especially tried to remember their names, so he could use them when saying thank you. But the last presenter caught him off guard, and the diligent attention he'd given the other students, mutated to a dumbstruck stare.

"Hello, Roberto," she said. "My name is Linea."

Her voice was as gentle as quaking leaves, her skin almost translucent. A deep auburn braid fell across her shoulder; her eyes were as dark as his own. She was holding up his favorite drawing, a copy of the very one he had moved from the ceiling to a place of honor on the wall next to Buck.

"I drew the letter L for Lupine," she said. "The lower case is the stem. The upper case is here on the side, creating a frame for the flowers."

Robert stared and the others watched, amused at his obvious infatuation. Fawn was not amused. "Roberto!" she said, bluntly; he shifted his dreamy eyes toward Fawn. "We could use more sodas. They're in the back of the van."

After a moment's hesitation, Robert picked up the ice chest and, more like a zombie than a man on a mission, followed Fawn's instruction.

"Did I say something wrong?" Linea asked.

"No, of course not; I think lupine reminds him of home . . . nostalgia, that's all."

When Robert returned, he and Alan distributed the cake and party favors. To no one's surprise, and a bit to its maker's chagrin, Robert set Fawn's basket in front of Linea.

The last event was a piñata. Robert was given the job of holding the end of the rope. He lifted the purple, paper, capital P out of reach of every blindfolded batter's wild swings until Fawn took her turn. When she made contact, gold and silver chocolate kisses rained down like a meteor shower.

CHAPTER 24

"I can't wait for you to meet my grandmother," Fawn said. She and Robert were in the kitchen loading up day packs with water and food. Ever the instructor, Sonja walked in carrying two sets of binoculars and two identification books, one on wildflowers, one on birds.

"I think Robert will benefit from learning the names given to plants and animals in this region," she said.

It was the first day of summer vacation. Sonja had accepted Dan's offer of a job as counselor for the girl's six-week session at Muir Camp. Sonja was going to drop Fawn and Robert off at Isabelle's gate, then drive in to the farm, take their suitcases to the house, have a quick visit and be on her way. She'd tried to talk them into coming with her to camp, but Fawn, was adamant. "Mom, I want Robert to spend time with Grandmother. Who knows what he'll decide at the end of summer; there might not be another chance."

Sonja had reminded Fawn that after Robert participated in the boy's session at Muir Camp, coming back to live with them would be one of his options.

But Fawn had a feeling Robert wouldn't choose to return to Paso Robles. Sonja's demeanor made him uncomfortable. She'd tried to explain why Sonja acted the way she did. "My mom is a scientist," she said. "She compartmentalizes." Robert shook his head. "Words!"

"She cares about you, and she's committed to help with The Plan; she's just really pragmatic."

"Pragmatic?" Robert repeated. Just when he thought he had humans figured out, Fawn would try to explain another word, another confusing label of some aspect of "personality".

Undeterred, Fawn kept at it. "There are, of course, different definitions for pragmatic. In Mom's case it means practical, efficient, sensible . . . and I guess I should include hard headed, persistent and dogmatic."

"Dog?"

"No. Dogmatic. She has certain ways of doing things, and she's more comfortable with people who are like her."

Robert thought about this. "Me too," he said. "I like **you**."

Robert's innocent compliment made Fawn blush, but she knew he really meant he cared for her like a sister, and she was, almost, content with that.

Sonja raced out of the house shouting, "Fawn! Robert! Let's get moving. I have a long drive ahead of me." She hadn't realized that they had long since left the house and were loading their suitcases into the trunk.

Fawn leaned to the side and called, "We're already out here." An unusually flustered Sonja turned back to close and lock the front door. "She changed her outfit again,"

Fawn whispered. "I think Mom is hot for Ranger Dan."

Robert grinned. "Not pragmatic, now."

"You are so perceptive," Fawn laughed.

"Perceptive," Robert repeated. "I know it."

"Exactly."

Sonja slid into the driver's seat, adjusted the rear-view mirror, put the car in reverse and started to back out of the driveway. The emergency brake held tight, and it took a few seconds for her to realize she needed to release it. Robert and Fawn snickered.

"What are you two laughing at?"

"Nothing," they responded in unison.

Robert had taken his usual place in the back seat. They were a few blocks from the house when he overheard Sonja say to Fawn, "Dan and I talked last night. He suggested I take Robert to San Francisco straight from Isabelle's so he can catch a ride with the other boys headed up to camp."

A forceful "Stop!" from the back seat reminded Fawn of the Fresno fiasco. She whipped around to look at Robert. "What's wrong?"

"Not come back to Sonja house?"

Sonja continued to drive, but glanced briefly in the rear-view mirror to make eye-contact with Robert. "It's just logistics," she explained. "Dan can't come to get you, and it's much closer to take you to San Francisco directly from Fawn's Grandmother's farm than for me to make another trip to Muir Camp."

"Stop," Robert repeated. "Please."

Sonja let out an exasperated sigh and pulled over. She

turned around in her seat with the squint-eyed look that always made him uncomfortable. "Why?"

"Buck."

"Robert," she said, firmly, "Buck can stay in Paso Robles." In actuality, Sonja had already asked one of her neighbors to put Buck in a black plastic bag, stick him in the garage, and open all the windows in Robert's room.

Robert's reply was equally as firm. "No."

It's all he has . . . Dan's words kept her from refusing to back track, but did nothing to mollify her attitude. "Thank goodness we didn't get far from the house," she grumbled. Throwing the gearshift in reverse, she backed into a drive and pulled out right in front of an SUV. Breaks screeched and hands were thrown up in disbelief as the burly driver mouthed "dumb broad," (or blonde, Sonja wasn't sure) and sped away. Robert and Fawn didn't make a sound.

As soon as the car stopped in the drive, Robert sprinted up the walkway, grabbed the key from under a brick, unlocked the front door and raced to his room. He took his second skin from the closet shelf, spread it on the floor, lifted Buck's hide from the wall, rolled it and wrapped it with head and horns exposed. When he returned to the car, Sonja pulled a lever next to her seat. "Buck," she announced, "rides in the trunk."

As she and Robert stood at the gate watching Sonja's car head on up to Grandmother's farm, Fawn reflected on the last time she had stood there alone anticipating the twelve mile hike. Unlike the dull, dusty landscape that spread before her last September, the late spring lushness of the countryside, and a companion, made her incredibly happy. She sat down and removed her shoes. "Walking in barefoot was my father's way," she told Robert, and he immediately shucked his own.

"We walk in silence," said Robert.

The fruits of Silence are many: self-control, patience, dignity, reverence, courage . . . Grandmother's words; Fawn nodded.

The miles melted under their steady pace, and Robert began to feel relieved of the disquiet that had plagued him since he was thrown from Buck's back. At last, his sense of place was free of the endless distractions, from without and within, he'd experienced for the past ten months.

When they reached the top of the first rise, they stopped under a tree. Fawn immediately sat down and, lifting her foot as close to her face as possible, tried to spot what felt to be a deeply embedded thorn.

Robert took an apple from his pack and gazed at the view. When he noticed Fawn's contortions he was first amused, but then recognized she needed help. He sat beside her, handed her what was left of the apple and took her foot. He found the thorn, pulled it out and then rubbed the bottom of her foot until she assured him the problem had been solved.

"You are my knight in shining armor," Fawn said. "Oh, I'm sorry."

"Sorry?"

"I broke the silence."

"I'm okay," said Robert. "No distracted."

Robert never ceased to surprise Fawn. "Where did you learn that word?"

"Alan Chu," said Robert. "I distracted, miss ball. Before

human, no distracted."

Fawn made a sweeping gesture of the untamed terrain. "Not many distractions here. Lots of people think Grandmother should move into town, but she won't. She still lives the way most humans lived more than a hundred years ago."

"Hundred?"

"You know, counting, numbers." She took a stick and made hash marks on the ground. Although she slashed quickly it took some time before she completed twenty sets of five. "See these marks? Each one represents four seasons, one year. I have made one hundred marks."

Robert rolled his eyes. Fawn was amused, and a little remorseful, that he had learned to make what she and Sonja referred to as face crimes. "You must learn numbers," she said, seriously. "Humans are very interested in numbers."

It took a little over four hours to reach the top of the hill that overlooked Grandmother's little farm. With the goal in sight, Fawn started to run. When Isabelle hurried into her yard and waved, Robert held back to watch the reunion.

The woman below had rich brown skin and snowy white hair, woven like the hair of the women in the misty village. Fawn raced into her arms the way she had raced into Sonja's when they arrived in Paso Robles. Suddenly, the boy missed his first human teacher; he thought about Dan slapping him on his back the first time he put two words together. It had been his way of showing friendship, like the hugs Sonja had tried to give him. Fawn was waving at him now, and he started down the hill. When he got close, she took his hand. "This is my friend, Robert," she said. "Robert this is my grandmother."

The old woman looked straight into Robert's eyes, her gaze penetrating, yet kind. "Please," she said, "call me Isabelle."

"Isabelle," Robert repeated. "Nice - to - meet - you."

Isabelle was charmed by the young man's well rehearsed response, and couldn't help but notice her granddaughter beaming. They followed her through the garden and into the kitchen. "It smells good in here," Fawn said. "We didn't eat much on the hike. This guy travels fast."

"He does. I didn't expect you two so soon."

"Flicker not doing his job?" Fawn teased.

"He did his job. I said I didn't expect you so soon, I didn't say I hadn't had any warning. Everything's ready; let's eat."

Robert was grateful to eat in silence, but Fawn found she had to make that adjustment all over again. After a meal of rabbit stew, bread and salad, Fawn sailed up to her room to settle in. Isabelle showed Robert a small room downstairs where she had made up the bed for his visit. He thanked her for the offer, but said he preferred to sleep outside. The request was no surprise, and after he'd selected a place near the house between a sizable boulder and a small, sturdy oak where Buck could hang free, Isabelle furnished the space with a crock of fresh water.

The three soon settled into a comfortable routine, working in the morning and doing what they pleased on the hot afternoons. Fawn and Isabelle continued their basketry lessons. Robert explored the terrain and foraged for food, something he had not done since leaving Muir Camp.

Fawn and Robert had been at the farm for one month

when Isabelle asked the two of them to sit with her in the parlor after dinner. Accustomed to her consistently calm, positive demeanor, her somber tone took them aback. Had they done something wrong? After clearing the table they joined her in the cozy room. She had made special preparations for this meeting: A treasured hand woven rug was spread on the floor. In the north corner of the rug lay a white egret feather, on the south a chunk of black obsidian; at the east burned a tallow candle, at the west an abalone shell filled with water. She asked them to join her in the center of the rug and, following her instructions, the three stood with their backs together, facing out. Grandmother reached for their hands; Fawn and Robert completed the circle by joining their own. Grandmother's voice fell on their ears as a disembodied sound. "Our ancestors have called for communion. The time has arrived for us to make a vision quest."

The two listened carefully as Isabelle explained the ritual. The quest would begin with fasting; for two days they would eat only small amounts of raw vegetables, followed by three days of nothing but water. The culmination would be a journey to a sacred site of the ancient Esselen Tribe. Silence would be maintained throughout. "We will not wear shoes during this time," she told them, "but on the journey, we will cover our feet with deer hide."

"Buck," said Robert.

"Yes."

"When do we begin?" Fawn asked.

"Now."

Slowly they rotated one full circle, stopping briefly in front of each of the sacred symbols and then parted. Fawn and Robert returned to their private spaces feeling honored and humbled by what lay in store.

During the days of fasting, the three spent much of their time transforming Buck's hide into moccasins. To make the skin supple they rubbed it with hardwood ash, rinsed it repeatedly and soaked it in oily water. The skin was stretched over a smooth log to dry and, after scraping away the hair with a sharp stone, was ready to be made into the traditional foot coverings.

At dusk of the fifth day they left the farm, hiking late into the night by the light of a full moon, their destination a rocky crest of the coastal mountains. Well after midnight, each spread a blanket on the ground to rest; at first light they continued on. There was no sign of a trail, but Isabelle led the way without hesitation.

The sun was still hidden behind steep crags above when their leader disappeared. Fawn was momentarily confused, but Robert stepped in front of her, took her hand, and the two squeezed between two slabs of jagged rock that formed a nearly invisible, east facing passage into a cool, dry cave. Grandmother lowered herself to the earthen floor and began to chant. Robert and Fawn sat at her side, lending their voices to the deep, steady drone. The chant's undeviating rhythm was hypnotic. When a thin stream of light crept a few feet into the opening, hundreds of ancient Esselen hand prints appeared on the stone walls around them.

The boy was the first to stand. Unbridled by thought or desire, he was drawn toward a print with palm lines and finger joints as plain as his own. He centered himself, then mirrored his left hand a few millimeters from the distinct white shape. Rooted to the ground, he maintained the stance, hand unwavering, for several minutes. A dense energy field began to vibrate in the space between his hand and the prehistoric pigment. The message of the ancients awaiting him there came clear: *Telele ... You will inspire others by the manner of your being ... You are an instrument of light and, like the sun, you have the power to awaken those who are trapped in a nightmare of want and fear . . . Our spirit is bound to Mother Earth, she is our sacred home . . . We are with you.* Every cell in the boy's body absorbed the communication, nurtured his essence, strengthened his resolve. After expressing his gratitude, he returned to Isabelle's side and took up the chant.

Fawn, too, was called to center herself in front of one of the prints. As she neared the singular mark, she saw that its thumb had the same unusual shape as her own, a physical anomaly that deepened her sense of connection to the human being who, thousands of years before, had placed a hand on this wall of stone ... *My daughter, Source has blessed humankind through the gift you possess. You may trust your ancestors to support and protect you as you fulfill your destiny of service to all creation.*

Finally Grandmother Isabelle rose. She positioned herself at the center of the cave, raised both hands and slowly swept them in front of the field of prints in affirmation of the wisdom her ancient kin so freely offer to all who seek their council . . . *Good woman, you have been faithful. It is time. Let all be known.* After a period of contemplation, Isabelle placed her hands on her heart, then lowered them to her belly and with slow, measured steps walked out of the cavern.

Fawn and Robert brought the chant to a close. When they turned toward the light, they could see Grandmother standing straight and strong in the warmth of the sun. She greeted them with a smile then, digging deep into a pocket of her skirt, she presented three juicy peaches. Every small bite of the sweet, moist fruit was savored, each seed tucked into a pocket, and honoring their vow of silence, they trekked back to the farm.

The day after the vision quest, the three gathered at the table for a hearty breakfast. When they'd finished, Fawn asked if she could skip morning chores to work on her basket. "I can't believe Mom will be here in just a few days. I really want to get it done."

Grandmother and Robert went into the garden. Row by row they tended the vegetables for over an hour before he asked a question he'd held inside since he and Isabelle first met . . . "Do you know who I am?"

The lines of Isabelle's face deepened; her eyes were suddenly moist. She inhaled, then exhaled as if she were letting go of much more than a simple breath. "I do," she said. "You are the son of Lyle Stone."

"Did you know Lyle Stone?"

"I knew *of* him; Lyle Stone is the son of my deceased husband and a woman from the north." Free of the long kept secret, Isabelle unburdened herself, knowing her honesty would be a gift to the young man at her side. "My husband," she said, "went with other women. Your Grandmother was one of those women. She raised your father near her people in Monterey."

"Alive?"

"No."

"Esselen?"

"Yes."

"Sonja know?" Robert asked.

"I've never revealed my husband's secrets to anyone. I learned about Lyle from a letter I found after my husband died."

Robert put an arm around Isabelle; she rested her head on his shoulder. "I saw," Robert said. "Fawn and I are same."

"Yes, your fathers were half-brothers; you are part of the same family." Isabelle lifted her head and looked into the boy's deep brown eyes. "Sonja told me what The Council wants from you," she said. "It is a daunting assignment."

"Daunting?"

"Difficult."

"I know difficult."

"I'm sure you do. You will have many friends to support you, Robert, and I will be one of them."

"Thank you, Isabelle."

"You may call me Grandmother."

Learning they were cousins deepened the relationship between Robert and Fawn. Not only did they share blood lines, they both had lost their fathers. Sitting together at the top of Little Hawk Hill, Robert inquired gently, "My father falls from tree . . . your father?"

Fawn had avoided thinking about the day her mother drove into the yard and rushed toward the house frantically calling for Isabelle. The memory was all too vivid . . . the near hysteria in Sonja's voice when she said, "Robert's been shot," the hauntingly accurate imprint of the tortured look on the faces of her mother and grandmother.

She'd been sitting on a pile of catalogs stacked on a kitchen chair; Grandmother had just finished braiding her hair. Woven into each braid was a red ribbon to match a new red dress spread out on her bed upstairs. As soon as Father got home they were going to a party at a neighboring farm. All morning she had tingled in anticipation of the music, the games, the mounds of food and, best of all, lots of kids to play with. Before breakfast she and Grandmother had picked a gunny sack full of white corn and three huge watermelons. Father was going to hitch up Sage and Randy; they would ride to the party in the old buckboard. She would sit next to him and sometimes take the reins; he'd promised.

After Sonja's outburst, the two women she looked to for guidance stood silent and still. In the vacuum of that shock there was no sound, no color, no air. She'd attempted to break the seal by asking her mother to come upstairs with her to see the dress, but Sonja had not responded. Finally, Grandmother lifted her off the stack of catalogs, set her on the floor and suggested she go to her room and put the dress on . . . and she did. She remembered being very careful not to disturb the ribbons in her hair and, although unable to manipulate the buttons at the back of the dress, she'd managed to tie the sash and returned to the kitchen confident that her father would arrive any time. Later, in a fit of confusion and rage, she had torn the ribbons from her hair and stuffed the dress in the corner of the closet.

Her father was gone; mourning lay like a heavy fog over the house for months and months. Her mother cried, her Grandfather drank, her Grandmother gardened and cooked and cleaned and wove baskets to sell in town.

When she was older, her mother explained that her father was working with a group trying to outlaw drilling off the coast of California. There was an investigation, but never enough evidence to bring charges.

"My father was shot," she told Robert.
"Like Buck," Robert said.
"Yes."

Four days later Sonja drove away with Robert in the passenger's seat. She was taking him to San Francisco where he would board a bus full of boys bound for John Muir Environmental Camp. Fawn had decided to stay at the farm for the rest of the summer. Watching Sonja's car disappear, she could not hide the sadness she felt at seeing her best friend go.

Isabelle put an arm around her granddaughter's shoulder. "He will always be your family, Fawn," she said, "and mine."

CHAPTER 25

A glaring heat penetrated the windshield as Sonja and Robert drove away from the farm. The growth beyond Isabelle's garden was as dry as the parched earth protecting its tenacious roots. Sonja glanced over at the young man in the passenger's seat, turned on the air conditioning and settled back. *Look at him,* she thought. *How had she not seen it before? He was a young version of her husband, her Robert: the serious brown eyes, the strong determined jaw, the slightly protruding left ear . . . just like Fawn.*

When she drove up to the farm yesterday, she'd sensed something had changed. Isabelle, Fawn and Robert, stood side by side in the dusty road to greet her, smiling, waving, a triumvirate newly formed. At the dinner table they excitedly pressed her for details of her adventures at Muir Camp and, after being stuck in the car alone for so many hours, she'd enthusiastically recounted "Tales of Sonja, the Intrepid Camp Counselor." The finale to her melodrama brought a blush to her cheeks. "Dan and I," she confessed, "enjoyed each other's company very, very much."

Along with knowing smiles from the younger set, that bit of news had prompted Isabelle to stand up, kiss the top of her head and say, "This calls for dessert!"

They'd insisted she sit while they removed the dinner dishes, and soon there was a pot of tea and a fresh berry pie on the table, waiting to be served. When everyone returned to their places the three exchanged glances, but no one moved or spoke. The air of expectation was palpable. Confused, Sonja had asked, "Should I pour the tea?"

Fawn had looked to the others and then, grinning broadly, blurted out, "Robert and I are cousins!"

Once the announcement was made, Fawn and Robert sat on the edge of their chairs and launched into an animated narration of the events of the past nine days: the preparation and ceremony of the vision quest, Robert's forthright question, Isabelle's forthright answer, Fawn's reaction to the news – at first surprised, but after she thought about it, not surprised at all.

The pie sat untouched for over an hour while the four of them poured over old photo albums and memorabilia. "Holly and Lyle, and Robert and I worked together for a whole summer," Sonja said. "Look, here's a photo of the four of us at the beach in Santa Barbara distributing information about off-shore drilling." Robert and Fawn leaned in to inspect the photo, both impressed by their father's similar grins.

"Lyle and Holly were quite a few years younger than Robert and me," Sonja continued, "but we shared the same interests, and like everyone in the environmental movement here, they admired Robert tremendously." She settled back into her chair and sighed. "Two years after this photo was taken, Holly and I were both pregnant." She took a thoughtful sip of her tea, then looked toward her mother-in-law. "Isabelle, you haven't said much for awhile."

When Isabelle finally spoke, her tone was unusually terse. "Why didn't you or my son tell the authorities there was a baby in that tree?"

It was an obvious question, one Sonja had grappled with many times. She wondered if her answer would make sense after all these years. "Holly and Lyle were dedicated to staying where they were until California Electric agreed to save the old growth redwoods ... and they were adamant no one expose the fact they'd had a baby. He was healthy, doing fine, but Holly was convinced Child Protective Services would take him away. Fawn was just a few months old then; Robert and I understood how she felt and," she looked directly at Isabelle, "we made the decision to respect Holly and Lyle's wishes." Beginning to tear up, Sonja lowered her head and wiped her eyes with her napkin. "Sadness and joy are all mixed up in me right now," she said. In the silence that followed, Robert reached for Sonja's hand. The discomfort she'd sensed every time she tried to hug him had made the gesture all the more meaningful.

The solemn mood had shifted when Isabelle offered dessert for the second time, and the evening ended on a sweet note. When it was time for bed, Robert chose to sleep in the house so they would all be together, the whole family, safely under one roof.

**

While Sonja was occupied with last night's revelations, Robert was engrossed in the breath taking views of the rugged California coast. To his left, rolling breakers crashed against mammoth rocks near the shoreline; to his right, steep canyons, enticingly lush and verdant, shot up from the road. He didn't seem to notice when a sensor went off on the dashboard. Sonja pulled over at the next opportunity and shut off the car.

As soon as they stopped, Robert reached for the door handle. "I go there," he said, pointing out the window.

"Yes, of course," Sonja said. "It's time to take a break. Don't be gone too long; it's at least another three hours to the city."

The boy sprinted up hill, out of sight, and Sonja rolled down the window to let the sea breeze clear her head. The sensor vibrated again; P3 was close, very close. As with all of the condors, she logged in sightings of him monthly, but they had not communicated since that night, nearly a year ago, when he tapped on her window, the night Fawn had shifted and gone to Muir Camp for the second time.

As soon as she got out of the car, Sonja heard the whoosh of his enormous wings and spotted him gliding toward a substantial rock outcropping on the ocean side of the highway. Hurrying across the road, she stepped over the guard rail and, head down, made her way on all fours along a narrow ledge a few feet below road level. When she reached a place where the ledge widened she stood and looked up; there he was, regal and elegant as ever. As soon as their eyes met, communication began.

Greetings, friend . . . I see you are taking the boy north.
"To San Francisco."

P3 explained he'd initiated their communication for a specific purpose; The Council wanted details of the boy's progress, and Sonja was confident they would be pleased with the information P3 would take back to them. "He and Fawn stayed six weeks at Fawn's grandmother's house. The boy found his human roots in the Esselen tribe. It has made him very happy."

This is good.

She added more specific information. "Dan brought him and Fawn to Paso Robles five moons ago so he could experience a larger human population. His language skills are improving. Tomorrow he will return to Muir Camp with boys his own age." She sensed P3's approval. "Do you want to have contact with him now?"

No, I do not wish to disturb him. But there is something I need to make clear. Sonja watched P3's eyes, carefully. *Touching the ground with bare feet is essential for the boy to maintain a balance between who he has been and who he is becoming. Do you understand?*

"Yes."

Then, to Sonja's surprise, P3 terminated their communication by closing his eyes, extending his glossy black wings and dropping off the cliff. The abrupt end to their meeting left her feeling empty. Back in the car, she reclined the seat and closed her eyes. Perhaps it was time she admit to herself that, like P3, her role in The Plan was rapidly diminishing.

Sonja knew she had rubbed Robert the wrong way; pushy teachers could be like that. But she also knew what he'd learned in the past few months was as vital for survival as knowing how to forage for food. He could communicate more readily, recognize his letters and identify some words. And, thanks to Alan Chu, play a mean game of tennis... He's ready for the country club! The thought made her laugh out loud.

Just then Robert opened the door and slid into the seat.

"Why laugh?" he asked.

"Because you are amazing, and I'm happy."

"Me too," he said.

"Good run?" she asked.

"It - is - beautiful."

"California's Coastal Mountains," she trilled, "hard to top it."

"On globe is this mountains," Robert said, "and mountains where I come tomorrow."

Sonja nodded. Admittedly, Robert's language skills needed work, but she understood what he was saying, quite an accomplishment in a few months time. His new haircut and clothing accentuated his good looks; he'd gained height, a little weight and, if she looked closely, she could see signs of a mustache. He's as handsome and charming as his Uncle Robert, she thought, and pulled onto Highway One feeling like a proud auntie.

By the time they reached the bay area, commuter traffic was at its peak. Sonja turned on the radio; Robert gawked at the somber faces cooped up in moving dens. "Not beautiful," he said. But when the San Francisco skyline came into view, he was intrigued. "Go there."

"That's where we're headed." Sonja had booked a room at a small hotel in North Beach. Her plan was for them to walk in the city that night and do a little sight-seeing by car the next day before meeting the bus at the Ferry Building. After checking in, the two walked down to the financial district, but the older ornate buildings, and even the modern glass ones, didn't hold Robert's interest. Next they hiked up Nob hill toward Grace Cathedral. "This building is called a church," Sonja continued. "There are different kinds of churches. In Christian churches you will see that symbol." She pointed to a cross.

"Lower case t," said Robert.

Relieved of an inquiry to explain the symbol of suffering, Sonja said simply, "That's right."

From Nob Hill they took the cable car back down to North Beach. Robert thoroughly enjoyed the ride, leaning out to the side as far as he could and relishing the rhythm of the conductor's bell. Back at the hotel, Sonja urged him to try one of the twin beds. "You'll need to sleep on a bunk in a cabin with the other boys," she reminded him. He tried, but couldn't stop squirming and before long, he was fast asleep on the floor.

Early the next day the two explored Golden Gate Park and walked in the Japanese Garden, climbing over the high arched bridge, strolling around a large pond with water lilies, and colorful koi. They drank tea overlooking a graceful brook where small birds splashed and then darted toward the tea house to snatch up crumbs left from sweet almond cookies.

Robert spotted a large statue of the Buddha set back from the main path. "Who?" he asked.

"The Buddha," Sonja said.

"Quiet man, yes?"

"Yes."

"I like quiet."

When they returned to the car, Sonja glanced at the clock on the dash; they had just enough time. She drove to the parking lot near the Golden Gate Bridge. "Let's go." Robert nodded and leapt from the car.

They walked to center span. The water sparkled, seagulls swooped and squawked. Angel Island, Alcatraz, the bay bridge, sailboats, freighters and the San Francisco skyline were spread before them like a child's elaborate play set. The view kindled a perspective Robert had not fully experienced until that moment . . . *the variety of human experience appeared to be limitless.*

He could barely contain his excitement.

CHAPTER 26

Alex Perry paced in front of the Ferry Building waiting for other campers to show up. Even though the bus was scheduled to arrive at 1:30, he'd walked out of the house with his duffel and sleeping bag well before noon. His folks could hardly believe he wanted to attend another summer session at Muir Camp.

Marjorie was propped up in bed reading when he went to her room to say goodbye.

"I'll bet you'll be the oldest camper there," she said.

"I'm used to being the oldest."

"That's what happens with a December birthday. I was just the opposite, always the youngest in my class."

"You've talked about that," Alex reminded her.

"Oh. Well, don't you want to eat lunch before you go? Hector can give you a ride; he must be done with the roses."

"I feel like walking."

"Then give us a kiss," she said. "I won't see you for six whole weeks!"

Alex dutifully pecked his mother's cheek. "Have a

good time, Mom, with … whatever you do while I'm gone. See you when I get back."

Alex looked at his watch, 1:20. Scanning the multiple lanes of traffic on the embarcadero, something unexpected caught his eye; that's Sonja Henderson, and she has a kid with her! He watched her park her car opposite the Ferry Building then deftly negotiated his way across the wide thoroughfare.

Sonja and a boy about his own age were taking a duffel and sleeping bag out of the trunk. "Sonja," he called, "I thought I recognized you."

"Alex. Hi, I was hoping to see you here."

The kid stuck out his hand and Alex took it, impressed by the firm grip. "My name is Roberto Muniz."

"Nice to meet you. I'm Alex Perry. I know Sonja."

"I know Sonja," said Roberto Muniz.

"Roberto came to the U.S. from Mexico," Sonja explained. "He needed surgery to correct a hearing issue. A church in Paso Robles was his sponsor, and he's been living with me for a few months." Robert was staring so intensely at Alex, Sonja felt compelled to shift his focus. "We've been working on language skills, haven't we Roberto."

Robert shifted his gaze to Sonja; she was obviously expecting him to say something.

"Yes," he said, hoping he'd chosen the correct response.

"I thought camp would be a good experience for him," Sonja continued. "Could you show him the ropes?"

"Right up my alley," Alex replied.

"Thanks," Sonja said. "That would be great; this is all new to him, the culture, the language."

"No worries."

Sonja reflected on her quick exchange with Alex: show him the ropes, right up my alley, no worries; phrases like that would roll off Robert's tongue before long. He was staring again, but Alex didn't seem uncomfortable. Robert was in good hands. In just a few hours he would be back in familiar territory with Dan close by. It was time for her to leave. She opened her arms and was pleased when Robert accepted her hug without reservation. "Goodbye, Roberto," she said. "Keep in touch."

Robert kept an eye on Sonja's small white sedan until it disappeared into the distance. "Come on," Alex said, "let's take your stuff and set it by mine." Robert picked up his duffel, Alex grabbed the sleeping bag.

As they monitored the traffic, looking for a break between the sea of automobiles, bikes and buses, Robert asked, "What is keep touch?"

"Keep **in** touch," Alex said.

Robert poked his duffel . . . "Touch."

"That is touch, but **in** touch is different," Alex explained. "Sonja wants you to let her know how you are doing. Usually you could give her a call or send an e-mail, but at Muir Camp we're not allowed to use electronics, so you'll have to write her a letter."

"I do not write."

"No problem," Alex said. "I've got it down; I'll help you."

"Got it down," Robert repeated.

"That means I know how to do it really well." Alex couldn't believe what was coming out of his mouth…letter writing? He'd only done it when forced by his parents, but he could actually imagine enjoying the process if it would help Roberto.

"You live in city?" Robert asked.

"Yes."

"Golden Gate Park?"

"I play tennis there sometimes."

"I play tennis," said Roberto.

Alex flashed his broad grin. "Maybe we'll get to play sometime."

Robert beamed. "Yes!"

Their stilted conversation charmed Alex. Roberto's unselfconscious eye contact, his naiveté, his absence of bravado was refreshing. This new, unexpected friend would lend a whole new dimension to the Muir Camp experience.

"Let's go," Alex shouted. He darted into the street, zigzagging through the creeping traffic. Undaunted, Robert took off behind him and was soon ahead, leaping over hoods of cars in a straight shot toward the Ferry building. When he reached the side walk, Robert looked back; Alex was standing on the median, glaring at him.

"That was quite a show you put on," Alex said when he reached Robert's side. If the long, deep blast of the Alcatraz Ferry's air-horn had not diverted Robert's attention, he might have been curious about the steely cast of Alex's ice blue eyes.

As more boys arrived, Alex took charge of introductions. "This is my friend, Roberto."

Robert smiled and shook hands with the firm grip Alan

Chu had taught him. While the pace of conversation kept him silent, he paid particular attention to the display of body language. His creature mentors had accepted him as a serious student of their methods of survival, and he had managed to overcome many of his human limitations. Still, the vast differences between himself and his adoptive families were always apparent. But in the midst of this group of boys, he had no doubt he could become adept at mimicking the behaviors of his own species.

As soon as he spotted the bus, Alex grabbed his duffle and sleeping bag, urging Roberto to do the same. They were first in line, and Alex made sure they sat in the front seat to the driver's right. "This is the best view," he said, but his real motivation for choosing the seat was to have Roberto to himself. Roberto was *his* project, *his* student.

**

Dan scurried around the camp, checking to make sure everything was ready. At Sonja's suggestion he had hired a bus to transport the campers to Muir Camp. It was expensive, and he decided the families would still be responsible for picking the campers up at the end of the session. But her idea made the schedule for orientation and dinner predictable; the boys would be filing off the bus anytime now and "Roberto" would be one of them

.

Sonja had called after dropping Robert off at the Ferry Building. "It's going to be fine," she told Dan. "Alex was right there when we drove up. Roberto introduced himself without a hitch and, I've got to say, Alex seemed genuinely excited to meet him."

"Roberto, Roberto, Roberto," Dan repeated. "I've got to get that through my head."

"Don't worry about it," said Sonja. "Robert, Roberto, it's no big deal. If the campers hear you call him Robert, they'll just think you're getting old." There was plenty of affection in her tease.

When the bus arrived, Dan instructed the boys to check the bulletin board for their cabin assignments and stow their gear before gathering for orientation. He had put Robert in the same cabin with Alex, Nate and Fee, thinking familiar faces might be less threatening. When Alex excitedly introduced Roberto to Dan, Robert showed no trace of recognition.

Roberto looked quite different from the Robert Dan had taken to Paso Robles. Sonja and Fawn had done a great job of making him look the part: hair professionally cut and styled, a brand new shirt with the Nike logo and sturdy, sandals. The shorts, however, were the very ones he'd removed from the clothesline almost a year ago. Dan watched him head for the cabin with his three mates. They were like stair steps: Alex, the tallest, then Nate, (whose roundness had stretched into height,) Roberto, and lastly Fee (who seemed not to have grown at all since the winter retreat.)

Nate and Fee took the bottom bunks; Alex and Roberto spread their sleeping bags up top.

"We don't have to go to orientation do we?" Fee said.

"No, just the newbies have to go," Alex answered, "but I'll take Roberto; he might need a little interpretation. Roberto is just learning to speak," he said casually.

"You mean he's just learning English, right?" said Nate.

"I speak Spanish, you know."

"No, really, he's just learning to speak," Alex said. "He was completely deaf, living in Mexico and some church group brought him to the states for corrective surgery."

"How'd he get lined up to come to camp?" Fee asked.

Alex began digging through his duffle for a sweatshirt and was beginning to wonder if he'd forgotten to pack it. "He was living with Sonja Henderson, you know, the girl's counselor at the winter retreat. She set it up."

Robert had been sitting on his bunk while Alex told the story of Roberto, perfectly happy not to repeat the decoy. Nate looked up at him and asked. "Was it fun to live with Sonja?"

"Yes," Roberto replied. "Fawn is my friend."

Alex's searching came to a halt; he couldn't believe what he'd just heard. "Did you say Fawn?"

"Fawn is daughter, Sonja is mother," Roberto said, plainly.

A trio of voices. "What?"

Fee was almost indignant. "How come Fawn didn't tell any of us they were related?"

Nate weighed in. "She probably didn't want people to think she was tagging along with Mommy."

Fee's eyes squinted behind his thick glasses. "Wait a minute," he said. "I'm pretty sure when Fawn found me she used the same two-fingered whistle I'd heard Sonja use earlier that day. Jeez, I should have figured it out."

Alex felt betrayed; he'd ridden in the front seat of the van all the way back to San Francisco and, for some reason, Sonja had kept up the act. *Never trust* – that lesson always seemed to come when he least expected it. "It's not like they look alike," he said. "I mean, who would have guessed. Come on, Roberto, I'll take you to orientation."

At dinner that night, Roberto loaded his plate with grilled chicken and mounds of salad. He sat next to Alex, chewing slowly while the other boys ate and talked. After dinner everyone gathered at the Native Peoples village, each sitting on a round of oak log while the counselors led them in games designed to bond the group. They ended the evening by roasting marshmallows over the campfire, and the boys tromped off to their cabins in high spirits.

Alex, Nate and Fee talked for nearly an hour before falling silent. Robert stared at the ceiling of the cabin, diving beneath the drone of conversation to focus on the smells and sounds of Black Oak Forest, faint now in the wake of his cabin mate's scents and chatter. He immersed himself in the memory of sleeping on the floor of the sweat lodge with Buck keeping vigil, and drifted off to sleep.

CHAPTER 27

Any reservation Dan had had about Robert's success at Muir Camp soon fell away. The boy seemed fully focused on becoming an all American-teen. Alex's tenacious tutoring had propelled Roberto's social and language skills to new heights. Sometimes he even wondered if "Roberto" had forgotten about Robert. But when he heard the rumor circulating through camp that Roberto had been seen in unusually close proximity to several wild animals, Dan knew the boy hadn't given into fragrant soap, shampoo or deodorant, a distinct advantage when it came to approaching wildlife. Of course his awareness of wind direction, and an affinity for moving through the forest without a sound were in his favor, too. No, he thought, the boy is still here.

Alex hadn't forgotten Roberto's daredevil sprint across traffic on the embarcadero. When a volleyball or basketball game was proposed, he made sure Roberto was on his side. Skilled in cooperation, Roberto learned quickly to set Alex up for slam dunks and ferocious spikes. They were a team unto themselves, and when Alex flashed a smile of appreciation toward his new friend, Roberto felt confident his reintroduction was, at last, a success.

As it often did this time of year, the temperature spiked to 104 degrees five days in a row; the energy of campers and counselors alike began to flag, and the afternoon schedule was changed to give the boys more time to loll in the shade or swim in the pool. Roberto's athleticism had been noticed by a couple of competitive swimmers attending camp, and they'd set out to teach him the four common stokes: free, back, butterfly and breast. He was on his way to see if a practice lane was free when Alex sprinted up to propose a different plan.

"Let's go to the stream; there's a swimming hole beyond the meadow. If we hike to it by water, we'll be in the shade the whole time. Not only that, there's tons of ripe berries all along the bank, and huge old grapevines hang from the trees. It's really amazing."

It was not Alex's sales pitch, but the unavailability of a swim lane that made Robert amenable to the idea. He'd felt his success at adaptation would be hindered if he revisited the past and had avoided the areas of camp he'd retreated to last fall when the pressure of reintroduction had become too intense.

They walked down the entrance road past the meadow and ducked under the guard rail at the bridge a half-mile down-stream from the swimming hole. Here, with Alex at his side, the memory of their first encounter was palpable; Robert could almost feel the bark of the broad oak limb under his belly as he watched Alex remove his second skin and foot coverings before plunging into the water.

To Alex's surprise, Roberto stripped down and set his clothes and sandals on the bank. Sure, Alex had skinny dipped a few times last year but, jeez, they were right below the road! After a moment's hesitation, he stripped down too, stashing his clothes and new water shoes under the bridge where no one would spot them. He knew he should have asked permission to take the hike and now, buck naked, he was even more anxious to round the first bend where they couldn't be seen.

Without water shoes, walking on the rocky bottom was more difficult than Alex had expected; Roberto, however, seemed unfazed. Alex searched for a sandy spot to sooth his already tender feet. He found the perfect place near the bank where Roberto was already reaching into cascading vines to pluck berries by the handful.

"Ahhh," Alex crooned as he lowered himself into the water, "now this is paradise." He dunked his head and threaded his fingers through his hair. Looking up through wet lashes, he thought he saw something crawling up Roberto's leg. He rubbed his eyes and looked again – was that a spider? "Roberto! There's something on your leg!"

Robert calmly swiped at the place Alex was pointing to and resumed harvesting the dark, purple fruit. Alex picked his way over to get a better look. "What's that mark?"

"Mark?" Roberto stretched around, trying to see what Alex was talking about. "I can't see."

Alex squinted. "It looks kind of like letters"

"Letters?"

"Yeah. Two Rs, an A, and a . . . B; it's weird."

"Don't know," Roberto said. His apparent disinterest made Alex wish he'd taken a closer look before making such a big deal. Either Roberto actually hadn't known about the mark, or was self-conscious about it – It *was* pretty strange, like an amateurish tattoo.

Much to Alex's relief, they didn't move very far for the first twenty minutes. But when they began to hike toward the swimming hole in earnest, he stared down constantly, always searching for a little sand between the rocks. He heard the sound of gushing water and looked up briefly to where the stream poured over tall, granite boulders, but he was so pre-occupied by his aching feet, he didn't notice the deep pool at the base of the fall. All at once, he was in over his head with a torrent of water pushing him down.

When Robert saw what was happening, he grabbed a thick grape vine dangling overhead and, anchored by the vine, he leaned over the pool, pulled Alex out and shoved him hard toward the shallows. Alex fell onto the rocks, a miserable landing, and began coughing uncontrollably. When he recovered, he looked up to see Roberto scaling the boulder, using the vine like a rope to pull himself hand over hand to the top.

The scene struck Alex like a waking dream. He forgot his aching feet, and when Roberto tossed the vine to him he grabbed it, swung across the pool, gripped the rough granite surface with his bare feet and climbed up to join his friend. *He'd climbed rope in gym class lots of times, but this! This was the real thing!* Never in his life had he felt so in touch with his body, never so at one with Nature. Standing tall on top of the boulder, he looked downstream, pounded his chest and let out a Tarzan yell.

Roberto laughed. "Sound like coyote."

Alex hollered again. "Feel like Spider-Man."

"Spider-Man? What spider-man?"

"He's a character . . . in a movie."

"Movie?"

"You've never seen a movie?"

"No."

"Wow, that's amazing." Alex smiled. "I'd really like to be there the first time you do see one."

"Okay," said Robert.

"Movies, by the way, are ubiquitous," Alex said, quickly reclaiming his teacher status.

"U-what?"

"Ubiquitous. It's a ten dollar word. It means everywhere. Words like that make a good impression. I can teach you all about making a good impression." With that, Alex faced upstream, and seeing deep silt at the base of the boulders, he took a bounding leap.

"Oh, shit!"

"Shit," Roberto echoed.

"Forget I said that."

Blood billowed through the water as Alex limped toward the bank. He sat down, examined the wound, and pulled a piece of broken bottle from the bottom of his foot. Roberto immediately scaled the bank and disappeared, returning moments later with a handful of slender green leaves. He held them out to Alex with a grin. "These," he said, "are ubiquitous."

"Great," said Alex.

"Chew," Roberto ordered.

"Are you kidding me?"

"Chew."

Alex ground the leaves with his teeth, not pleasant, but not too bad. When Roberto held an open palm in front of his mouth, he spit out the masticated pulp and shut his eyes while Roberto pressed the gooey mass onto the wound.

"Stay," Roberto ordered and took off again. This time when he returned he was dressed and carrying Alex's clothes and water shoes. Alex put on his shorts and Roberto helped him keep the makeshift poultice in place while easing the injured foot into the tight fitting shoe.

"What's that stuff you put on my foot?" Alex asked.

"Poultice," Robert answered. "Fawn's grandmother teach me."

Ah, Fawn, Alex mused, the pipsqueak who had stolen his thunder at the retreat. He'd nearly forgotten about *that* connection.

As soon as they reached the swimming pool, Roberto claimed a vacant lane, and Alex headed up to the first aide room. The walk back had been surprisingly painless; maybe he wouldn't need stitches.

"Sit right up there," the nurse said, indicating a gurney-type table. "So, you cut yourself?"

"Yes," Alex answered.

She turned her back to him and began gathering supplies. "Didn't have those shoes on when you got that cut, did you."

"No ma'am."

"I assume you know the rules."

"Yes, of course," Alex said, "but, you see, I was with

my new friend, Roberto. Have you heard of him?"

"Can't say that I have."

"Well, he's a little different, challenged in a few areas, poor family; he didn't even have water shoes."

The nurse raised her eyebrows and let out an exaggerated *I've heard it all before* sigh. Alex concluded his excuse, saying, "I was worried about making him feel bad, so I decided to go barefoot, too. It was foolish, I know."

Unimpressed by Alex's attempt to charm, she set cleansing wipes, antibiotic cream, bandages, a roll of gauze and some adhesive tape next to him and began to examine the bottom of his foot. She pinched the poultice between her thumb and forefinger and held it up. "And what in the world do we have here?"

"Roberto comes from a little village in Mexico; he knows about herbal medicine. He gave it to me to chew and then put it on the cut. It took the pain away, I'll give it that."

The nurse wrinkled her nose. "Disgusting." She threw the wad in the trash and then made a show of thoroughly washing her hands.

Alex knew enough to stop talking while she ministered to his wound. Since the water shoe would never fit over his bandaged foot, she wrapped it in a plastic bag and handed him a boot for sprained ankles.

"Go to your cabin, and put on shoes and socks. Bring the boot back tomorrow. I'll need to change the dressing everyday to make sure there's no infection."

Alex slid off the table. "Thank you."

He'd almost made it to the door when she announced, "I'll be reporting this to Mr. Fisk. You are to stay out of the pool, and the stream, for the rest of the season."

"Damn it," Alex said under his breath.

"Watch your language young man!"

"Excuse me, ma'am. It's just so very, very hot."

She smiled. "There's a reason for rules, you know."

**

Sonja's last words to Robert seemed to have slipped his mind or, more likely, he had no way to honor them. Keeping in touch wasn't easy for an illiterate boy. She gave Dan a call.

Dan was filling out the daily log of events when the phone rang. "Dan Fisk," he announced.

"Hi Dan, it's Sonja. How's he doing?"

"Actually," Dan said, "it's fortuitous you called this evening. It has been going really, really well until just this afternoon. I had to call Roberto in for a little chat."

"Why?"

"It seems he and Alex decided to shuck their shoes and get into the stream at the bridge with the intent to hike in the water all the way up to the swimming hole."

"Just the two of them?"

"Yep. It's been over a hundred degrees for days, so we decided to give the boys a free afternoon. I guess those two thought the pool was too crowded. At any rate, Alex stepped on some glass in the stream and managed to get a fairly deep cut on the bottom of his foot. The nurse reported it and emphasized the mandatory shoe requirement. Alex told her he went barefoot because Roberto didn't have water-shoes. I had to let Robert know, in no uncertain terms, he wasn't to go barefoot again."

"He hates shoes," Sonja said.

"He seems okay with the sandals you bought, and I

found a pair of water shoes in the lost and found that will work. Looks like Alex will be staying out of the pool for the rest of the session though."

"That reminds me," Sonja said, "I forgot to tell you something. I saw P3 when Robert and I were driving up to San Francisco."

"Did Robert see him?"

"No. I have a sensor in my car. When I realized P3 was near, I pulled over just south of Big Sur. Robert asked if he could take a hike, and since I didn't know if The Council was allowing contact, I told him to go ahead. After he took off, P3 landed on a rock outcropping on the ocean side of the road; I met him there. The Council is still adamant Robert move forward without interruption from any of the creature community, but they wanted an update."

"And you had a lot of good news," said Dan.

"Yes, P3 seemed pleased. But just before we parted, he made it clear that touching the ground with bare feet is essential for Robert to maintain a balance between who he has been and who he is becoming."

"Sonja," Dan said, firmly, "I can't exclude Robert from the shoe rule. Our insurance policy requires it."

"I understand; it's just that . . . "

"The other boys will leave here in a few weeks, then he can go barefoot again."

"Or he can come to Paso to live with Fawn and me. He can go barefoot here, a lot of the time, anyway."

"Or you could come here and watch him go barefoot," Dan said.

"Or you could come here," Sonja countered, "and we could brave the next step in The Plan together."

Like parents, with obligations keeping them miles apart, they would have figure out how to share their "son."

**

Alex's foot healed quickly but, with the exception of a shower, the nurse would not budge on her order about staying out of the water. Roberto continued perfecting his swim strokes and making more friends. Alex had to deal with a level of possessiveness that surprised him. Alone in the lodge one night, he composed a letter he'd been thinking about writing for some time:

August 11, 2013

Dear Father,

There is a boy, a cabin mate of mine here at Muir Camp, who came to the U.S. from Mexico sometime in the past year. I don't know all the details, but I do know he was born deaf, or at least really hard of hearing. A church group sponsored him to come to the U.S. for corrective surgery. He ended up living in Paso Robles with a woman named Sonja Henderson, one of the counselors at the winter retreat, and she arranged for him to come to camp this summer.

I have helped him with his English, and he has become a good friend. I know this sounds impulsive, but I've always wanted a sibling, and I think he could use a home.

If this is something you would consider, you could start by contacting the head naturalist/ caretaker of John Muir Camp:

Dan Fisk,
P.O. Box 434,
Figley, CA 95381

Very truly yours,

Alex

CHAPTER 28

Congressman Perry's secretary sorted his mail into two piles, personal and business. Aides went through the business pile, setting aside the few communiqués Perry had to attend to himself. The rest were answered with form letters, form e-mails, form questionnaires, and the occasional form thank you/photo card.

This morning he sat down at his desk to look through the few pieces of mail that had been identified as being sent by friends or relatives. (He had, at one time, let Marjorie answer these, but lately she wasn't up to much.) As he flipped through the envelopes one from John Muir Environmental Camp caught his eye. Was Alex there again? . . . Yes, of course; Marjorie had mentioned the boy wanted to go one last time, surprising to get a letter though, never happened before. He ripped open the envelope and read the letter, not once but twice, then called to make an appointment with one of his advisors.

"Bill, Perry here. I just received an interesting letter from my son. He has a request that I think could help us

227

with the Hispanic vote. Can we meet at Charlie's this afternoon, say 3:00? . . . Good."

**

Alex checked the mail every day. In just one week he would be leaving Muir Camp. If only he'd written the letter sooner. With the amount of mail his father received, and the number of people sorting through it, there was a good chance it had been lost in the shuffle. When Dan asked him to stop by the cottage after breakfast, he hardly dared to hope it was about what he'd proposed. "What's up?" he said casually when Dan came to the door.

"I got a letter from your father. It seems you asked if Roberto could live with your family."

"My father got in touch with you?"

"Sounds like you're surprised."

At once, Alex was as hyper as the day he thought he'd seen a condor. Heart racing, he verbalized every thought that came into his head. "I've never written to Father from camp before. I was beginning to wonder if my letter fell to bottom of the pile; I mean, I mailed it two weeks ago, and I didn't think to put "time sensitive" on the outside. Wow, I can't believe he wrote back!"

Dan countered Alex's enthusiasm with a straightforward, "Your father has requested I research the feasibility of your idea."

Undeterred, Alex crooned, "I'm sooooo . . . " He didn't finish the sentence but launched off again with unbridled excitement: "We have a lot of room at my house – He could go to my school – We could hire a tutor." His voice rose with each declaration, a list he'd been making practically since the day he and Roberto met.

"Slow down," Dan cautioned. "Ms. Henderson will have a say in this and, most likely, other people too."

"You mean Sonja?"

"Yes. I'm sure she expects Roberto to return to Paso Robles after camp."

Minimally deflated, Alex said, "Roberto said he liked the city. Maybe he could just try a semester, see how it works out."

"I'll call Ms. Henderson tonight."

Regaining his balance, Alex offered his hand. "Thank you," he said. "It would mean a lot to me if Roberto could come."

After Alex left the cottage, Dan sat down on the edge of his bed and stared into space. This new development was as surreal as when he'd called Sonja out of the blue a year ago and she said she'd expected his call.

Fate, Destiny, W-Y-R-D, Dan thought. *God is alive, magic is afoot, magic never dies.*

It was ninety degrees in the cottage; a chill ran up his spine.

**

"It's exactly what The Council wanted. He'll be living on the inside track; it's the road to influence. Dan, you have to let him go." Sonja had that authoritative sound in her voice.

Dan started pacing. "I'm not saying he should stay here with me. I think he should live with you and Fawn for at least a couple more years; he's only thirteen."

"He's had the Paso Robles experience," Sonja said.

"Four months . . . That's nothing," Dan argued.

"You say he's integrated with the other boys; you've used words like popular and confident," Sonja countered. "The sooner he dives in the deep end, the easier it will be for him to float."

"Float? What the hell does that mean?"

Sonja lowered her voice, slowed the pace of her speech. "I mean he'll be comfortable with those kinds of people. He'll have a prep-school education, rub elbows with boys from families that could make a difference. That's what *The Plan* is about, Dan."

Dan was convinced his intuition was correct. Sonja was ignoring what he thought was obvious. "*Those* kinds of people," he said, "*use* people like Roberto. Congressman Perry doesn't do anything that's not somehow to his advantage."

"Forget that. Alex is a wonderful kid, and he's Robert's ticket to the next step. This is no coincidence, Dan."

"But – "

"Why don't we let Robert decide for himself."

The next day Dan summoned Alex again, this time explaining that Ms. Henderson was authorized to allow Roberto to live with his family but strictly on a trial basis. She also insisted Roberto make the decision. "I think I should be the one to tell him of your father's proposal," Dan said. "If he has any hesitation, it would be easier for him to tell me than to disappoint you."

"Of course," Alex agreed. "When will you tell him?"

"I've asked him to stop by on his way to lunch."

Roberto bounded into the lodge just as the campers were splitting into groups for the afternoon activities. Alex had lagged behind, keeping an eye on the door. When Roberto appeared, he bolted across the room. A spontaneous eruption of back slapping, bear hugging, and lifting each other into the air ensued. Nate and Fee exchanged confused looks and pressed for what news could cause such celebration.

"You're kidding!" Fee said. "That is soooo cool."

"Is he going home with you right when we leave camp?" Nate asked.

"Yes!"

"Yes," Roberto repeated. "I go to San Francisco to home."

Ever vigilant, Alex said, "I am going to San Francisco to live with Alex's family. Repeat."

Roberto smiled broadly. "Alex is correct."

The boys left the lodge to join the other campers on the lawn where four greased poles had been sunk into the ground. Lines were forming behind each one; there was much jostling to be at the rear, a distinct advantage. "Just remember," the counselor said, "hang on if you start sliding down."

Because Alex and Roberto were the last to get to the event, they had to go first and neither made more than a couple of feet up the slippery surface. After everyone had had a turn, they all had another go, the ones at the front of the line on the first try, getting the last spot on the second. The less greasy surface made it possible for several of the boys to get close to the top but, with no hand-holds or bark to grip, no one made it, not even Roberto, who flopped on the ground after his second attempt and laughed so whole heartedly tears flowed from his eyes – tears of joy.

CHAPTER 29

"Come on, Fee," Nate coaxed. "Archery is fun."

"I'm not strong enough to battle a bow."

"You're not going to get stronger lying on the bunk," Nate said. "Talk to the counselor, see if you can be one of the arrow pullers; it's like being the ball boy."

Fee and Nate joined the other campers on the wide shady lawn. Targets adhered to bales of hay had been set up at one end, stations with bows and arrows at the other. The boys lined up in groups to take turns shooting, each one getting three shots before the runners collected the arrows and returned them to the stations. Alex and Roberto had arrived early to help set up the targets, and Alex had taken the opportunity to show Roberto how to position the arrow, draw the bow, aim and release with a steady hand.

Knowing there would be a competition, Alex had been practicing at the park for a solid month before leaving for camp, and he easily maintained the lead for the first three days. By Thursday, Roberto had begun to perfect his technique; their scores were neck and neck. If Alex made a bull's-eye, Roberto would grin and give a thumbs up, while Alex struggled to suppress a building resentment when someone so new to the sport bested him.

Usually the boys talked until they went to sleep – Fee, Nate and Alex throwing playful verbal jabs back and forth between the bunks and Roberto doing his best to join in. But that night Alex rolled toward the wall saying he was "too tired for this stupid conversation."

Roberto stared at the tense torso in the top bunk across from his. The vibration of Alex's surly mood brought to mind the feeling he'd had on the night of the caged raccoons, those unrelenting words of doubt and frustration he could not control. He wanted to find a way to make his friend happy. As he puzzled over what to do, Fee and Nate's conversation gave him the answer.

"Nice guy, but can't stand to lose," Fee whispered.

"Yeah," Nate agreed, "probably has a shelf in his room for trophies; just gotta have that pine cone sprayed gold to add to his collection."

"I got a trophy once," Fee said.

"For what?"

"Chess champion, fifth grade."

"You play chess!"

"Obviously."

"Tomorrow after lunch," Nate said. "There's a set in the game cupboard. Man this is great."

"Yeah . . . I hope you don't stop talking to me though," Fee teased. "I'm a monster when it comes to chess."

On Friday, only the top fifteen archers competed – four

rounds, three arrows each time. After the first two rounds, Roberto and Alex were tied for first place, but during the last two, Roberto fell behind, with one arrow missing the target completely. In the end, Alex walked away victorious.

When Roberto walked over to give him a congratulatory slap, Alex asked, "What happened?"

Roberto held up his hand; Alex grimaced at the two raw, broken blisters.

"Bummer," said Alex, "takes time to build up calluses."

After dinner, awards were handed out for the competitions held that week. Alex strode up to accept the "golden" pine cone in a classy yellow shirt. He knew if he won his photo would be included in the awards scrapbook; he'd brought the shirt just in case.

"You'd think he was accepting an Oscar," Nate whispered.

"Well," Fee said, "you've got to admit, he looks the part. Some guys get all the breaks."

After the awards Fee and Nate stayed in the lodge to play chess; Alex and Roberto returned to the cabin. In a gesture of comradeship, Alex asked to bandage Roberto's blisters. "The nurse gave me extra stuff. I think she was tired of seeing me every day. Sit right there," he said, indicating Felix's bunk. Roberto sat and Alex arranged the antibiotic cream and bandages on the mattress between them. "Okay, hold out your hand."

Alex examined the oozing red sores, then looked again more carefully – The location of the broken blisters was all wrong. He kept his head down for a moment, then glared at Roberto. "You bastard! What the hell did you do to yourself?"

Anger, terror, and jealously contorted Alex's features into a vicious snarl. "You've made me into a chump," he screamed. Throwing the cream at the wall, Alex stormed out of the cabin.

Roberto felt sickened. He waited a while, then decided to take a hike, hoping to find Alex before dark – It was the yellow shirt that caught his eye. Alex was kneeling behind a boulder in the forest above the meadow; he held a bow and arrow. The champion archer positioned the arrow on the taut string and then, to Robert's horror, he stood, pulled, aimed and released. The arrow found its target, the slender hip of a yearling. The deer did not fall and, as Alex readied a second arrow, it disappeared into a mass of thick brush. The angry hunter threw the bow on the ground, shouted a word Roberto had not heard before and started back toward the camp.

**

The boy tracked the trail of blood into the thicket. When the trail became less obvious, he stopped to listen for a sound that would direct him toward the wounded animal. *Telele* . . . He swung his head swiftly to the left . . . *Telele*.

It was lying on its side. The angle of the drooping arrow seemed to have staunched the bleeding. When it saw him, the wounded animal tried to stand but was so weak, its head barely left the ground before a labored breath forced it to lower it again. The boy sought eye contact, and for the first time in nearly a year, he entered the sacred space of empathic awareness with another creature. He visualized removing the arrow and applying pressure to the wound with his hand, and the yearling remained completely still when he duplicated the steps. The crimson swath at the end of the arrow showed the puncture to be a palm-width deep. Fortunately, there was no barb to further tear the flesh; after a few minutes of steady pressure, the bleeding stopped. Hurrying to the stream, he dipped tightly cupped hands into the water and returned to offer a cool drink. When the rough tongue lapped the last bit of moisture, the boy briefly laid his head against the deer's side and left it there to rest. With luck, it would rise again before a hungry predator found its hiding place.

**

When Roberto returned to the cabin, Alex was sitting, head in hands, on the edge of Fee's bunk. As soon as he saw Roberto, he wiped his eyes and started for the door.

"Enough," Roberto said, firmly.

"What do you mean enough?" Alex growled. "Don't you ever pull that kind of crap again, you hear me!"

Roberto simply stared at the enraged boy. "Enough," he repeated. "Sore hand is decoy; you are my friend." He extended the injured hand. "Shake?"

The shock of Roberto's refusal to engage in conflict completely disarmed Alex. He left the cabin but returned shortly after dark to sleep. The incident wasn't mentioned again, nor did Roberto reveal what he had seen. In time, he began to wonder if he had dreamt of the wounded deer and the brief resurrection of his former self.

**

Isabelle tossed-and-turned and finally rose from her rumpled bed. What had she done? After all these months of working with Fawn and then with Robert, of coming to grips with her long held secrets and rejoicing in the fruition of their efforts, she'd broken her own rule and given way to Fawn's plea for permission to shift.

News of Robert's decision to live in San Francisco with Alex Perry's family had put Fawn into a spin. "I just want to go to Muir Camp before he leaves. Who knows if we'll see him again? He might even forget us."

Isabelle remembered assuring Fawn that Robert would always be family, but who really knew. He'd be living in a world of mass distraction. Former connections could easily be overshadowed, even buried, as he adapted to his new life. Her resolve had softened; she had opened the door of possibility just enough to allow Fawn to convince her that a quick visit would be perfectly safe. In the end, she'd ceremoniously gathered the necessary implements to send Fawn on her way.

Wandering in her moonlit garden, she hung on to Fawn's last words. "Don't worry; I'll be fine. I'll stay near the camp buildings. There's no danger there."

Oh Great Spirit, where is she? Was it time to notify Sonja?

**

Fawn drifted in and out of consciousness. Each time she attempted to move, excruciating pain sent her back into a fitful dream state. When she awoke after dark, her instincts told her she was in danger; her bloody scent would surely beckon nocturnal predators. Her heart raced, a pounding pulse ached deep in her flank. HELP – HELP – HELP ME!

Her pleas were silent, but her call was answered... *You may trust your ancestors to support and protect you as you fulfill your destiny of service to all creation* ... Her Esselen kin embraced her. They touched her heart; the beat slowed.

They touched her wound; the pain subsided. They were chanting now, and Fawn aligned herself with the undeviating rhythm. It was the stable foundation she needed to focus her intention to return to human form.

At last, she felt the feathery tingling in her chest; it radiated out through her neck, her head and extremities. Falling into the blessed weightlessness and gentle rocking, she was laid to rest near the fragrant tomato vines in Grandmother's garden.

Isabelle sat amongst bolting chard and drooping vines. She had nearly fallen asleep when she heard Flicker screech. The startling noise alerted her to a much more subtle sound; Fawn's unconscious whimpering led her to a limp body collapsed against the chicken coop. Hurrying into the house, she returned with lantern, blanket and pillow. She spread the blanket on the ground, rolled the semi-consciousness girl onto it and slipped the pillow under her head. Fawn's skin was amazingly pale, almost translucent. Isabelle examined every inch of the girl's body; apparently, a puncture wound on the right hip had caused a significant loss of blood. Before going to the kitchen to brew blood-strengthening herbs, the old woman whispered into her precious granddaughter's ear . . . *You are home, Fawn . . . you are safe . . . you will recover.*

CHAPTER 30

The schedule for the last day at camp was always the same: breakfast, free time, pool party and barbecue. While Alex, Fee and Nate were busy rolling up their bags and stuffing their duffels, Roberto decided to run over to Dan's cottage to ask if he could keep the water shoes.

"Sure," said Dan. "Glad you could use them." He turned toward the counter and poured himself a cup of coffee. "You must be excited about living in San Francisco."

"Yes," Roberto replied.

Dan walked to his desk, retrieved the scrapbook he had made and handed it to Robert. "This is for you."

"What is it?" Roberto asked.

"Something you might enjoy when you learn to read."

"Thank you."

"I want you to . . . " Dan began.

The boy held up a flat hand. "Enough."

Dan duplicated the signal.

Looking deep into Dan's eyes, the boy said, "Teacher, I am okay."

Dan watched Roberto walk away. The young man's pronouncement told him his part in The Plan had come to an end. The apprehension he'd felt when confronted with the responsibility of taking charge of the wild boy was nothing compared to the disquiet of this painful goodbye. While he grappled with sentimental attachment, he knew Robert looked toward the future with optimistic anticipation.

Going into the bathroom, Dan glanced at the partially open window, Robert's secret escape route during the winter retreat. A myriad of reminders of the boy he had come to love would play on Dan's emotions in the months to come. He closed the window, washed his face and left the cabin to finish his duties on this last day of the 2013 season at John Muir Environmental Camp.

**

Alex tried to convince Roberto to take a final hike before they had to leave, but Roberto chose to spend time at the pool; swimming had become his activity of choice. Still banned from 'recreational waters,' Alex went along anyway. The counselors and some of the campers were busy lighting barbecues and setting up a table with condiments, chips, salads and desserts. Ice chests filled with sodas were carried to pool side. After watching the others horse around in the water, Alex had a stroke of genius, a way to participate. He rang the dinner bell to get everyone's attention.

"Hey, let's see who can swim underwater the longest without coming up for air." He held up his arm. "I'll use my watch for a timer. The winner gets the watch."

"You're on!"

The pool emptied, and a group of about twenty gathered on the deck at one end of the pool; a spectator section formed at the side.

"I'll need an assistant," Alex announced. Nate volunteered and pulled a pad and pen out of his pack. "Okay," Alex yelled. "Looks like lunch is close to ready; let's get this show on the road."

Roberto was first in one of the groups of swimmers lining up at each of the five lanes. Alex told them to call out their name before they dove in; Nate would keep track of how long each swimmer stayed under. As soon as someone took a breath they had to get out of the pool and another swimmer would take the lane.

"Roll call," Alex yelled.

"Justin – Eli – Sam – Cale – Roberto."

"On your mark, get set, go!" The race was on.

The first boy in lane three popped up before getting to the end. "Hey," the next in line yelled. "When do I start?"

"As soon as he gets out of the pool," Alex called, "and don't forget to call out your name."

Several of the swimmers made two lengths before taking a breath, a few made three. In less than six minutes every swimmer was out of the pool ... except one. The spectator's mouths hung open in amazement as Roberto continued to glide through the water. Arms extended straight in front, he propelled his body with his legs functioning as one unit, in a fluid up and down motion. The dinner bell rang, but no one moved.

One of the counselors walked over to Alex. "What's going on?"

"Eleven minutes, ten seconds," said Alex.

"Sure." the counselor replied. "I think that prize watch of yours is malfunctioning."

**

The boy gazed through the sunlit water. His eight-year old self was swimming with a colony of beaver. Together they were moving stones and branches to build a dam. Then more branches, pushing them into the muddy bottom, a reserve for winter nourishment. As the spirit moved him, he circled near the surface, dove, floated nearly to the top and dove again.

**

"Come on, it's time to eat. Get him out of there," the impatient counselor ordered.

"Don't worry, he's okay," Alex said. "Look, he's still swimming."

"Now!"

Nate handed Alex his pad and pencil and plunged into the pool. As soon as he touched the boy's skin, Roberto expelled the last of his air and rose to the surface.

Only a spectacular distraction could have diverted the rapt attention of those observing the underwater feat . . . Congressman Perry had arrived.

CHAPTER 31

Dan couldn't seem to pry himself off the bed. After Roberto's visit he led a short meeting with the staff, went back to the cottage, positioned a fan to blow directly on his body and laid down. He'd never given way to worry, had chosen an uncomplicated life. The arrival of the boy could have been complicated, but the kid was so independent and capable, worry didn't enter the picture. Concerns? Sure. But Sonja had soothed those with long phone calls, assurances, good advice . . . Sonja.

His eyes grew heavy; he hadn't slept well since Perry's letter arrived. The counselors could take care of the rest of the day. Reminding himself to appreciate the good things in life, like the noisy old fan cooling his sweaty skin, he drifted off to sleep.

"Dan! You'd better get out here!"

Dan leapt from the bed. One of the counselors was peering through the screen door, and hot on his heels was a man right out of an Eddie Bower catalog, a young woman with a microphone and a guy with a camera.

"Whoa, whoa, whoa," Dan repeated. "What's going on here?"

"You must be Dan Fisk."

The visitor was well over six feet, perfect haircut, even tan and an *I've got the world by the tail* smile.

"And you must be Mr. Perry." Dan pushed open the screen. "Come on in. The place is small; it's probably better if your friends wait outside."

"Fine," Perry responded. "Jen, Tom, you two go on over to the pool. Take some shots of the kids. I'm sure the counselors have a few interesting stories."

Before the assistants could get away, Dan stepped onto the porch. "That's against our policy, Perry. Muir Camp is technology free. You're staff is welcome to some lunch, but no photos, no interviews. These kids are under eighteen; invading their privacy will be prosecuted."

"You heard him," Perry said, curtly. "This won't take long. I'll see you in a few minutes."

Dan held the screen open and the congressman stepped into the cottage. "I'm sure you understand these boys are my responsibility," Dan said.

"Of course," Perry replied. "But I'm doing a generous thing here. I don't see why you're trying to make me look like a chump."

Perry was bristling, and Dan felt a tad smug watching him work to regain his composure. "What can I do for you?"

"I have papers."

"I'm sure you do," Dan said. "Have a seat. How about a glass of water?"

Perry sat down, cleared his throat. "Yes. Thank you."

Dan filled a glass and set it on the table. "We have our own well here; I think you'll taste the difference."

Perry had opened a briefcase and was sorting through two sets of papers. "I brought copies of Sonja Henderson's release," he said. "You'll note it specifically states a six-month trial period. If the boy is a fit, we may go for adoption; that remains to be seen. We just need your signature here acknowledging the agreement and your permission, as head counselor, for us to take him from the camp."

Dan picked up the pen, stared blankly at the document, and signed his name.

"Apparently," Perry continued, "Henderson is a member of the church that brought him to the U.S. It seems his family of origin is difficult to contact ... illiterate." He gathered the bulk of the papers and slipped them into his leather briefcase. "My lawyers are all top notch. Neither you, nor she, can be held responsible; I made sure of that."

"That's considerate."

"He'll be perfectly safe with my wife and me . . . and Alex, of course."

"Of course."

Perry pointed to the papers he'd left on the table. "That's a copy for your records." He pushed his chair back, stood and guzzled the water. Setting the glass firmly on the table, he said, "Well, I guess that's it." He scanned the room, made his appraisal; "I used to dream of living in a place like this . . . before I grew up," and walked out the door.

Dan picked up the glass. It was all he could do not to throw it across the room. Instead, he walked to the trash can and chucked it in – hard. There was no satisfying break, so he fished it out, washed it, dried it and set it next to the other three he kept on the shelf. Someday, he and Sonja, and Fawn and Robert would sit at his table – and he'd still have a matched set.

Perry strode down to the pool. His aides had already left in their own car. His driver stood near the barbecue, hot dog in hand, chatting with one of the counselors. Alex and Roberto ran over to greet him.

"Father," Alex said, "this is Roberto."

Roberto stuck out his hand, "Very nice to meet you."

Perry shook the boy's hand and was pleasantly surprised by the firm grip. He was also pleased with the kid's camera appeal – *Thank God he's good looking.* "All right you two," he said, "we're finished here. Get your things together. I'll be in the parking lot."

The driver took another hot dog, said his goodbyes and followed the boss. "Sir," he said when he caught up with Perry, "Are you hungry?"

Perry glanced back, grabbed the hot dog and downed it in two bites.

The Congressman and his driver sat in the front seat of the limo. "Start the car," Perry said, "and turn up the air." He removed a handkerchief from his pocket and wiped his brow. "I can't believe anyone would choose to live in a place like this." Glancing toward the main part of camp, he spotted his son and the Mexican kid shuffling across the dusty lot. He lowered the window and yelled, "Pick up your feet," and immediately pushed the button to raise it again.

Roberto watched Alex's father's face disappear as the window moved back up in one smooth motion. "Big car," he said.

"Yeah," said Alex, "comes with the territory. We won't have to ride in it much. We can walk all over the city or take the bus."

"I like it," said Roberto.

The chauffeur stepped out to help load the boys' gear, then opened the door to the back seat. Roberto admired the fine upholstery, the plush carpet, the glass panel that separated them from the men up front. Alex reached into a burl-wood compartment and pulled out an i-pod.

"What's that?" Roberto asked.

"Check it out." Alex put the ear phones on Roberto's head and selected a song. Roberto's reaction was priceless, wide eyes, big smile; in moments his head was bobbing.

Congressman Perry flipped the visor down and used the mirror to check on the boys. Roberto already had Alex's i-pod -- *Lucky kid.*

The driver was easing the limo down the gravel road when he saw a broad shadow sweep across the scarred expanse; he leaned forward. "Congressman," he said, pointing to the sky, "is that a condor?"

Perry glanced out the window. "I doubt it; condors don't live in the Sierra." He flipped up the visor and sat back. "Probably a turkey vulture; there's a lot of them up here . . . plenty of road-kill."

The driver continued to stare at the huge bird gliding above the tree tops. "It's sure a big one."

"Keep your eyes on the road."

"Yes sir."

**

Condor soared above the limousine for a few miles, then circled back to perch in a tall pine that held an abandoned heron nest. He'd wait for the cover of darkness before heading home.

The End of Book One

RRAB

The adventure continues . . .

Spring Equinox, 2018

Midnight. Robert sat on the narrow walkway that encircled the top of the lighthouse on Alcatraz Island. He had sought refuge here often in the past five years. Blissfully alone, he avoided the dazzling illumination of the San Francisco skyline and gazed at the stars.

He'd made his first escape to Alcatraz only two weeks after his arrival in Pacific Heights. Sneaking out of the bedroom he shared with Alex, son of Congressman Phillip Perry and wife Marjorie, he had sprinted down-hill to the marina, stripped and hid his clothing beneath the pier. Slipping into cold black waters, he dove under and covered several hundred yards before surfacing.

That first swim to "The Rock" set the precedent for every other; after popping up, he would start with freestyle, flip over for the backstroke, then complete the trip with the breast stroke, gliding cautiously toward the rocks where he would make his landing. During the swim, he never failed to recall learning those strokes in the pool at Muir Camp the summer before moving to the city. It seemed to him now that he'd had plenty of warning that summer, should have sensed the discord to come. But, in truth, being human was so new to him then that he couldn't have predicted what the next five years would bring. Oh, sweet naiveté. The word made him smile; he had quite the vocabulary now, thousands of words – and to think he'd managed a full, rich life without any of them.

Robert loved this tower of peace and quiet, the only sound the slap of water on rocks or the occasional squawk of a seagull late to roost. He thought of Fawn, that time in Paso Robles when she'd marched him up the hill in back of Sonja's house and pointed to a rusty metal sign in her first attempt to justify the importance of learning to read. "See this," she'd said, "It says NO TRESPASSING - VIOLATORS WILL BE PROSECUTED." Oh, the irony; the same sign was attached to the fence he scaled each time he came to this island.

His after-dark excursions were more risky now than they had been in the beginning. Several times over the past five years, there had been sightings. At first it was just a paragraph buried in the paper somewhere . . . 'Police were summoned to Union Square at two a.m. Wednesday when several citizens reported seeing a figure climbing up the side of a building. Officers could not corroborate the story and, given the fact that the witnesses were obviously inebriated, no report was filed.'
    He had spaced his forays into the night with irregularity and variety of location, but a few days ago he'd spotted a bold headline in the Weekly Enquirer that gave him pause – **BIG FOOT SPOTTED AT AT&T PARK!** He'd let a

number of shoppers go in front of him while he flipped through the pages, looking for the article. 'Several residents of South Beach reported seeing a bulky ape-like figure walking around the top of AT&T Park. Paulette Grimes, spokesman for the San Francisco Giants, denied it was a publicity stunt.' Robert chuckled to himself . . . *Big Foot. That's a good one! – Do I want to get caught? – No.* It was time to put the prankster to rest.

In less than two months, he and Alex would graduate from Belvedere Academy. Marjorie was planning a huge party. The Perry's were proud, very proud. Alex, slated to be the class of 2018's Valedictorian, had been accepted at Harvard, and their adopted son, "Roberto," would attend Cal Berkeley on an athletic scholarship.

Visit **www.beinghumanthebooks.com**
to sign up for updates on
upcoming novels in this series.

ABOUT THE AUTHOR

C. Nielsen Taylor lives in
Port Townsend, Washington
and Sonora, California.

Made in the USA
Charleston, SC
31 October 2015